THEY CAME TO SEATTLE

Scott Winslow—A jaded gambler and former U.S. Deputy Marshal, he took the biggest risk of his life to avenge his father's murder.

Kate Harrow—Despite the constant danger, she led a stage full of women across the vast Rockies to the Northwest's new world of opportunities—but doubted she would ever find a satisfying love for herself.

Matt Cord—Disguised as a wagon master, he was really an escaped murderer who killed without guilt and without warning. Now he planned to betray the unsuspecting settlers in his most savage crime yet.

Red Feather—A bitter renegade, he led a band of warriors who shared his burning drive to make the white people suffer.

The Stagecoach Series
Ask your bookseller for the books you have missed

STAGECOACH STATION 7:
SEATTLE

Hank Mitchum

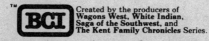

™ **BCI** Created by the producers of
Wagons West, White Indian,
Saga of the Southwest, and
The Kent Family Chronicles Series.

Executive Producer: Lyle Kenyon Engel

BANTAM BOOKS
TORONTO · NEW YORK · LONDON · SYDNEY

STAGECOACH STATION 7: SEATTLE

*A Bantam Book / published by arrangement with
Book Creations, Inc.*

Bantam edition / August 1983

*Produced by Book Creations, Inc.
Executive Producer: Lyle Kenyon Engel.*

ISBN 0-553-23428-5

Published simultaneously in the United States and Canada

PRINTED IN THE UNITED STATES OF AMERICA

O   0 9 8 7 6 5 4 3 2

STAGECOACH STATION 7:
SEATTLE

Chapter 1

Less than a mile south of Baker, a muddy little town in the foothills of Oregon's Blue Mountains, a stagecoach lurched through a pass, then plunged down a narrow, treacherous road that had been carelessly carved along the steep cliffside of the mountain. Filled to his collar with whiskey and hurling curses like thunderbolts, the stage driver again and again sent his bullwhip cracking out over his team's heaving, sweat-glistening backs.

Hanging on desperately beside the driver, a white-faced fellow in dark bowler hat and frock coat had long since given up trying to get the driver to slow down. Now he kept his eyes shut tightly and clung to the low iron railing beside him as the stage, like a ship plowing through heavy seas, rocked wildly on its mad course.

At times, less than a foot separated the coach's spinning wheels from the abyss as the stage careened around sharp bends and hurtled down steep grades. Far from hauling back on his reins at such moments, the whiskey-crazed driver seemed bent on increasing the pace. Occasionally an exultant cry would erupt from his throat, and

1

he would take another prodigious gulp from his flask. Aware though he was of the unhappy passenger beside him and the other equally terrified passengers hanging on below, he continued to urge his steeds to still greater speed. And by now the four scrambling horses—wild-eyed, nostrils flaring in terror—seemed intent on only one thing: escaping the mad fury of their driver.

A sharp curve appeared. Beyond it the driver saw only the peaks of distant mountains as the road abruptly dropped away. Reaching for his whiskey flask, he let out a yell, stood up in his box, and sent his whip snaking out over the flanks of his maddened horses.

Inside the plunging stagecoach, Kate Harrow was furious. Braced in one corner with her terrified girls huddled around her, she hung on for dear life, her mouth a straight, angry line, her dark emerald eyes smoldering. She, too, had long since given up her cries of outrage directed at the driver.

Dr. Braden Throckmorton was up there in the box alongside the driver, she knew. Suddenly, above the ear-splitting rattle of the coach, she thought she heard the doctor shouting down to her. She managed somehow to stick her head out the window. Glancing up, she caught sight of Throckmorton. He was pointing down the trail. She looked and saw what appeared to be a town, its buildings nestled in the heavy embrace of two small mountains. Baker! They were almost there!

Pulling her head back into the stage, she did her best to comfort the three girls. Not long after, an unpainted frame shack flashed by the window, and then another. Suddenly they were cutting onto a narrow, rutted street. Peering out the coach window, she saw a town that gave her very little comfort. Few of the frame buildings had seen a paintbrush or were likely to see one in the near future, and nearly every structure's sagging ridgepoles and

2

weathered, warped walls bore mute testimony to the mean winters so common in this windy corner of the Pacific Northwest.

The street that ran between the buildings was little more than a muddy trail. Fronting the street was the usual cluster of businesses: a blacksmith shop, a barbershop, a funeral parlor, a saloon, a general store, and a post office. And in the distance, across from the saloon, Kate could make out the town's only hotel—an unpainted, rambling, two-story affair toward which their drink-sodden driver was attempting to point his lathered team.

Scott Winslow looked with patient weariness across a table in Baker's lone saloon at the sallow squint-eye who was trying to bluff him. The squint's name was Lester Terman, and he already had lost more than he could really afford. Yet here he was trying to bluff Winslow again. The two other players tossed in their hands and leaned back to watch.

"That's right," Lester said, moistening his dry lips and shifting nervously in his seat. "You heard right, Winslow. I'll match you, and I'll raise you." He shoved into the pot all the chips that were left in front of him, then peered up at Winslow, his eyes narrowing still further. He looked like a weasel getting ready to pounce.

If the effort to bluff were not so pathetic, Winslow would have laughed, but something about this mean excuse for a poker player warned him against even the suggestion of a smile. Like most such creatures who drifted into the seamy little towns west of the Rockies, this one would sure as hell prove a mean and treacherous enemy if he were made to look too silly in front of his friends. With an easy shrug of his broad shoulders, Winslow counted out enough chips to see the man, then pushed them carefully into the pot.

3

Looking up at Lester, he drawled, almost gently, "All right, I'm calling you, Lester. What've you got?"

Heavy beads of perspiration were standing out on Terman's narrow forehead—he obviously hadn't expected Winslow to stay in. With desperate bravado, he threw down his hand.

Two pair. Jacks high.

Winslow found it difficult to believe Terman had stayed in and raised him with such a feeble hand—especially when he knew Winslow had kept three and drawn two, giving him at least three of a kind, for a winning hand. Careful that he not let his craggy face reveal the slightest trace of elation or show of triumph, Winslow dropped his hand face up on the table.

Full house. Aces and tens.

"Damn you!" Lester seethed. "You been winnin' too much! Let me see them cards!"

Winslow straightened, fixing Terman with suddenly cold eyes. "What're you looking for?"

"A marked deck, that's what I'm looking for!"

All conversation ceased. The sound of chairs sliding back filled the saloon. The barkeep stopped polishing his mahogany bar and slowly began to reach for the sawed-off shotgun he kept behind the counter.

With deceptive calm, Winslow picked up the cards he had just thrown down and carefully shuffled them into the deck. With equal deliberation, he collected the two other discarded hands and folded them into the deck as well. When he had a solid pile, he stood up and said, "Here's the deck. Be my guest—check it." And he flung the cards in Terman's face.

The deck struck the man sharply, exploding in a bright shower. As Terman reeled back, slapping at his six-gun, Winslow leaped across the table, grabbed the wrist of his gun hand, and twisted. Terman's howl of pain

4

filled the saloon as his weapon thunked heavily to the saloon floor.

Kicking the table out of his way, Winslow grabbed Terman's arm with both hands and swung him against the bar. After he slammed into it, belly first, Winslow spun him around and slapped him hard on the face, first on one cheek and then the other. The man's face purpled as tears of rage flooded his gray eyes. He started to protest, but Winslow was in no mood to listen. He spun him back around and with a well-aimed kick, sent him windmilling through the batwing doors of the saloon. A roar of approval greeted his departure.

Reaching down for Terman's six-gun, Winslow emptied the chambers and flung it out the door after him. Then he turned to the saloon patrons, who were watching him expectantly. "Drinks are on me!" he called out.

As the patrons stormed the bar, Scott Winslow reseated his gray Stetson hat, cashed in his chips, told the barkeep he would settle up later for the drinks, and headed for the door of the Loggers' Palace.

Six feet tall, lean, dark haired, and well tanned—despite the hours he spent gambling in the dim, smoke-filled saloon—there was an aloofness to the thirty-eight-year-old man, a weary contempt for the world that chilled most men. They liked him well enough, but kept their distance, uncomfortable with the cool gaze of his cobalt-blue eyes and the faintly sardonic smile of his wide, expressive mouth.

The trouble with Scott Winslow was that he had given up—on life and on people. He had long since discovered that no action was so foolish or so abominable that a fellow human wouldn't attempt it—at least once. Appalled and many times sickened by the behavior of his fellow men, he contented himself with the wry awareness that, at the very least, nothing ever surprised him.

A former U.S. deputy marshal, he was content to drift through the late autumn of 1863 in this dingy little town lost in the foothills of the Blue Mountains. What did it matter? What did anything matter? Far to the east a terrible war was pitting brother against brother, filling the creeks with blood and fouling the air with the stench of death. And into this far northwestern frontier, anxious to escape the carnage, fled the weak and the foolish, the dreamers and the fanatics. They didn't know what he had learned: Even up here in this pristine wilderness there was no escape from the assorted follies of mankind.

As Winslow stepped through the batwings of the Loggers' Palace, he knew he wouldn't see Lester Terman waiting for him. The little gray rodent of a man would already have found a hole somewhere in which to lick his wounded pride with whispered hate and promises of vengeance. He wouldn't try anything now while it was still light out. He would wait until dark.

But what Winslow *did* see surprised him more than Lester would have. Across the street, in front of the hotel, a stagecoach was lurching to a halt—the first stage he had seen since Indian trouble closed the Baker line nearly a year before.

As soon as the coach halted, Kate Harrow threw open the door and plunged out of it. Her eyes flashing in fury, she planted herself beside the stage and glared up at the driver. It was a good thing she was watching him, for the driver took one look at the ground, lost his senses, and toppled from his perch. As Kate jumped hastily out of the way, the inebriate landed heavily in the muddy street and lay where he had struck, barely conscious. He had missed her by inches.

Her arms akimbo, she glared down at the fallen driver, who somehow had managed to hang on to his whiskey flask.

Reaching down swiftly, Kate snatched the flask from his grasp, then emptied its contents over his prostrate form until the man was thoroughly soaked with alcohol. He groaned and tried to crawl away.

A crowd had gathered, and it greeted Kate's action with a raucous cheer. Glaring around at the leering faces, she flung the empty flask away, then looked back down at the bearded relic who several weeks earlier had pleaded for this job, promising he would stay sober.

"You're fired, Purvis!" she told him furiously. "You can stay in this town and rot, for all I care. Now get going!"

"But . . . but Kate . . ." the man stammered. "You can't do that. . . ."

"Yes, I can! And I'm doing it!"

The driver managed somehow to regain his feet. Well past fifty, he was as gaunt as a tree in winter. With a weak, pitiable flutter of his right arm, he reached out to Kate. She stepped back, allowing him to collapse forward on his face once again. He tried feebly to stand a second time, then lay still. Leaving him in the dust of the street, Kate turned back to the stagecoach.

A still-trembling Dr. Throckmorton already had climbed down and now was helping Kate's girls from the stage. Melody Tinsdale and Collette La Tour were close to hysteria. But not Terry Lambert. Her clear, intelligent eyes already were coolly appraising the string of tired-looking frame buildings that ran the length of Baker's single street.

"Over here, girls," Kate called out. "This hotel looks like it could use some business."

As she spoke, she led them imperiously through the encircling crowd and up the stairs onto the hotel porch. The desk clerk, who had hurried out of the hotel on the stage's arrival, and Dr. Throckmorton followed after with their trunks and luggage.

7

"Ma'am!" someone called from the crowd.

Kate paused before entering the hotel and turned, her eyes still smoldering.

"I own the livery stable," explained the fellow who had called out. "You want I should take care of the team and your stage?"

"Thank you," Kate said.

The hostler hurried over to the horses and started to lead the stage away.

"How you goin' to pay him for that service?" a bearded, leather-lunged fellow asked, drawing a raw bark of laughter from the crowd of grinning spectators. "You gonna pay in trade?"

Kate looked the loudmouth up and down for a moment, then said, "Well, mister, I don't think you'll ever have enough to gain my favor. But that gentleman has already earned my gratitude. Does that answer your question?"

As the fellow hastily looked away from her blazing eyes, his face reddening, Kate turned and led her girls into the hotel.

Watching from across the street, Scott Winslow was impressed—as much by the madam as by her three girls. Though everything about this entourage confirmed they were members of the oldest profession, Winslow saw in the madam a woman of quality and in her girls an intelligence and bearing that did credit not only to themselves, but to the madam as well. As the women entered the hotel, they walked erect, proudly. Though the dust of the day's journey and the press of their cramped quarters had left them somewhat disheveled, it was obvious their dresses were of the finest quality—with none of the garish fripperies such women usually sported.

Even more impressive to Winslow was the way they had handled themselves as they passed through the crowd.

The town of Baker was a lonely, woman-hungry outpost in the middle of nowhere. These men were desperate for the comfort of a woman—any kind of woman. A knowing smirk or a raised eyebrow from any one of the girls, and they would have been swallowed up. Yet throughout their short walk from the coach to the hotel, the girls had looked neither to the right nor to the left, coolly oblivious to the leering glances their presence had drawn from these men.

As the girls safely entered the hotel, Winslow smiled to himself at the look of relief on the beefy face of the single male member of the madam's entourage. He obviously had been fearful that the men crowding around were not going to be able to restrain their appetites. This worthy—an overweight, flabby-faced gentleman in his late fifties—was dressed with the threadbare pretensions of an indigent undertaker. Puffing unhappily as he lugged the girls' cases, he followed the desk clerk into the hotel.

As the crowd melted away from in front of the hotel and drifted back toward the saloon, Winslow crossed the narrow street, mounted the hotel stairs, and slumped into his favorite chair. Thumbing his Stetson back off his forehead, he leaned back against the wall and hooked his ankles over the porch railing just as a sharp scream came from the hotel lobby. Tipping his chair rapidly forward, Winslow jumped to his feet and ducked into the hotel.

The stout man who had been carrying the luggage was on the stairway wrestling with Bim Stagger, a huge bear of a man whom Winslow knew as a logger who occasionally came to Baker to quench his thirst for both liquor and women—and he never cared much about the condition or ancestry of either. Halfway up the stairs, Bim had grabbed one of the girls, and the portly gentleman in the frock coat was experiencing some difficulty in preventing him from carrying her off to one of the second-floor rooms.

As Winslow hurried across the lobby, Bim let loose with a ripping right jab and sent the older man tumbling backward down the stairs. With a furious oath, the madam rushed up the stairs after them—but she wisely held back when Bim paused and clenched a fist, waiting for her to reach him.

Infuriated, the madam turned and looked down at the crowd pouring into the hotel. "Isn't there one man among you leering hyenas? Will none of you help this girl?"

"What's the matter?" someone called. "You afraid you'll lose your cut?"

"Hell!" another cried. "She ain't in no danger of losing her virginity, is she?"

The remark drew hoots of laughter, and before it died entirely, a high piping voice in the back suggested that maybe a few of them should pick out girls for themselves—and then pass them around. It was a mean, witless remark, and it caused a hush to fall over the crowd. But it was a measure of the men's hunger that no one turned on the fellow who had made the suggestion.

Sensing the crowd's mood, Winslow pushed himself to the foot of the stairs and moved swiftly up them. He said nothing to the madam as he swept past her, and was just in time to see Bim shoving the girl into his room at the end of the hallway. Breaking into a run, he reached the door before Bim could close it all the way. With one well-aimed foot, Winslow kicked it open and charged inside. Bim flung the girl onto the bed and then turned to face him, a huge grin on his face.

"You want a turn with her, Winslow, you'll have to wait till I'm done. Else you'll have to answer to these." And he shook his big, hamlike fists.

Winslow moved in swiftly, feinted at Bim's head, then buried his fist into Bim's huge breadbasket. The punch rocked the man back and caused him to lower his guard. Winslow swung again and caught him flush on his cheekbone. The blow staggered Bim, but he just shook his head, lowered it, and rushed Winslow, intent on ramming him in the chest. Winslow slipped to one side and chopped the big man with devastating precision on the back of his neck. Dropping to one knee, Bim turned his head dazedly and glared up at Winslow.

"Damn you! She's mine! I saw her first! Go after one of the others!"

"It's this one I want, Bim," Winslow replied.

As he spoke, he planted a kick in Bim's rear end that sent him hurtling headfirst into the wall. With a groan, the man rolled over onto his back, cracked plaster showering over him.

Winslow turned to the girl, who had been cowering in a corner behind the bed. He smiled and reached out his hand to her. "Your madam is waiting for you," he said.

She got to her feet and moved carefully around the bed, glancing with some apprehension at the dazed logger.

"What's your name, girl?" Winslow asked.

"Terry Lambert," she said, moving swiftly past Winslow and out the door. Before she vanished, she looked back at him and smiled dazzlingly. "The madam's name is Kate Harrow. She'll want to thank you."

Terry was correct. A moment later, as Winslow pulled the door shut on Bim Stagger, the madam hurried down the hallway toward him.

"Thank you very much, Mister . . . ?"

"My name's Scott Winslow, ma'am," he said, reseating his hat more firmly on his head. "Miss Terry said you are Kate Harrow. I'm pleased to meet you."

She smiled. "I'm sure you must realize how grateful I am, Mr. Winslow. And the girls, as well."

Scott felt her sincerity and was immediately warmed by it. "I think they'll be all right now," he told her. "At

11

least, I hope so. I'll go see if I can scatter those animals downstairs.''

He touched his hat brim and hurried on down the hallway. An excited crowd was still milling around the hotel lobby. When the men saw him coming down the stairs, they knew at once he had prevailed. Several shook their heads, a few smirked, and the rest howled with derisive laughter.

''When you goin' to get your pay, Scott?'' cackled an old codger.

Winslow paused at the foot of the stairs and looked at the old-timer. ''A whole hell of a lot sooner than you will.'' Then his cold, contemptuous gaze swept the crowded lobby. ''A fine bunch of two-legged animals *you* are. Pigs at a trough have more dignity. Why don't you get the hell out of here? You must have something better to do.''

''Sure we have!'' someone in back called. ''For now!''

''Hell!'' another cried. ''This night ain't over yet!''

With that promise—and threat—the men crowded out of the lobby. Winslow followed them out and watched them disperse. Almost a dozen, he noticed, drifted across the street to the Loggers' Palace to fill their guts with alcohol and their timid souls with courage.

Winslow walked over to his chair on the porch and sat down again. He felt just a little upset with himself for getting involved in the affairs of an itinerant madam and her entourage. When he reminded himself of the mood Bim Stagger would be in for weeks to come he shuddered. It might have been smarter, he realized, to have killed the logger while he had the chance.

Baker had no law—no official law, that is. The cavalry sent men in regularly from the fort twenty-five miles to the southeast, but it did little good. Twice the job of town constable had been offered Winslow, and each time he had refused it. He knew what being a lawman entailed.

He had worked for a while as a U.S. deputy marshal, which was why the job had been offered to him in the first place. But that also was why Winslow had handed back the badge each time. Trying to keep the peace with a tin badge and a six-gun in this part of the Oregon frontier would be about as effective as pissing upwind.

Restless, Winslow got to his feet and started back across the street to the Loggers' Palace. Now that he was earning his bread by his skill at poker, it behooved him to keep in practice, he reasoned. And that fracas with Bim Stagger had left him a mite thirsty, as well.

Winslow had almost reached the saloon when a sharp yell caused him to glance up the street. A bearded settler, standing on his wagon's box, was cursing a team of exhausted horses as he whipped them down Baker's only street. The settler obviously had done nothing to spare his animals: Their flanks were flecked with foam, their nostrils flaring in terror. The wagon master was riding on horseback alongside, his back to Winslow as he turned in his saddle to wave on the five other wagons as they rumbled into Baker, heading for the campground on the north side of town.

Winslow was about to head into the saloon when the wagon master turned around in his saddle. In that instant, Winslow got a good look at the man's hard, chinless face—at the fellow's mean eyes especially. The shock of looking into those eyes caused Winslow to reach out and grab the saloon hitchrack for support. The wagon master was completely unaware of the reaction his presence had evoked. Glancing only casually in Winslow's direction, he rode on past the saloon and out of town, the dust of the wagon train gradually obliterating his image.

Stunned, Winslow straightened up and took a deep breath. At last he had found the man who murdered his father.

Chapter 2

Winslow was not a very good poker player that evening. After a few games during which he allowed his adversaries luck far beyond their expectations—he folded his hand, cashed in his few remaining chips, and retreated to a small table in a corner of the saloon, where he remained through the early hours of the evening, nursing a succession of beers. The grim set to his shoulders and the brooding intensity of his eyes warned away any of the saloon's patrons who might have sought his counsel.

It was not unusual to see Scott Winslow sequestered in this manner. Indeed, the saloon's regular patrons had come to expect such occasional behavior from the gambler, who seemed to observe the world through a cynical veil. But what Winslow felt in his heart this evening was not the simmering weariness of an existence he had come to hate. Instead he was feeling the sharp knife-edge of sorrow that had long lain dormant within his heart. Alive once again, it was eating at him with renewed vigor, threatening to topple the icy control he had held over his emotions for so long.

14

He had loved his father, a famous and highly regarded stage driver who had followed the stage lines west. To see Ben Winslow handle a team of six powerful steeds, his whip crackling like gunfire across the animals' heaving backs, was to see a god loose on this earth, driving a chariot straight from the bowels of hell. But this god—this man whom Scott Winslow would always remember with love and awe—had been struck down by a highwayman's bullet.

That highwayman was Mort Calisher. An enraged posse had apprehended Calisher, and after his trial Calisher had been sentenced to a life sentence at the prison near Fort Yuma, on the California border. But after less than a year, Calisher had escaped, and for three years now Winslow had been tracking him. A year ago, he had lost Calisher's trail in Billings, Dakota Territory, and since then had been drifting west toward the coast, gambling his way through town after town—a cold, remote figure whose shrewd bluffing at the poker table few could equal.

And now, suddenly, fate had dealt him a joker. Mort Calisher, the scum who had murdered his father, had just brought a wagon train through Baker. But Winslow had stared deep into those dead eyes and had done nothing. He should have whipped out his gun and blasted Calisher from his saddle. The wagon master would have been dead before he hit the ground, and Winslow's long search would have come to an end. He would have been able to go home at last.

But there no longer was any home for him to go to, and no reason to go if there had been. The hate that had scorched his gut for so many years had long since burned itself out. The loneliness and seeming futility of his interminable search had wrung him dry. All he wanted now was to find a place where he could escape the stench of his fellow men and watch his last sunset in peace.

Winslow picked up his stein of beer and shook his head. The gods must be laughing now as they placed their bets.

He finished his beer and beckoned to the barkeep. As he did so, he saw Kate Harrow push through the batwings. At once the saloon hushed. The handsome woman gave a quick, fierce glance around the room until she caught sight of Winslow. Swiftly, she strode toward his table. Winslow got up at once and pulled out a chair. She thanked him with a curt nod as she sat down.

"What are you drinking, Mr. Winslow?" she inquired. The saloon was still quiet, the patrons watching with bated breath and gleaming eyes.

"Beer."

"I'll join you then."

Winslow held up two fingers. The barkeep nodded, and a moment later he was hurrying across the saloon with two foaming steins.

"Here's to you, mister," the madam said. "Thanks for what you did back there. That logger was quite a handful."

With a curt nod, Winslow lifted the beer to his mouth and drank deep. He noticed that the madam drank almost as greedily, and he was just a mite amused at the unselfconscious way she wiped her chin afterward. Meanwhile, the quiet in the saloon lifted somewhat, and the clink of poker chips began to sound once more from the tables in back.

"To what do I owe this pleasure?" Winslow drawled.

"I need protection, Mr. Winslow," the madam said bluntly. "And this town doesn't seem to have a single law officer."

"That's true, it doesn't. There's a cavalry post down the river about twenty-five miles, but that war back east keeps draining away its manpower. Used to be, we could count on the cavalry to keep the peace in this region, but no more.''

"I know all about that terrible war back east, Winslow. But it's the war I have to fight right here in Baker that worries me.''

"You can call me Scott if you want," Winslow said, picking up his beer and sipping it.

"Thank you, Scott. And you can call me Kate," she said, allowing a smile for the first time since she entered the saloon. "But I still need some help, and I was hoping you would be it.''

"I sort of figured that was what you were driving at.''

"Will you help me?''

"What do you want me to do?''

"My girls—I am afraid for them. Three men have already tried to get past the desk clerk to the second floor, and one fellow offered a bribe to the poor man. The hotel owner told me not to worry, but it looks to me, Scott, that if push comes to shove, he isn't going to be much help.''

Winslow nodded. The owner of the hotel was Amos Brundig, a balding, bespectacled old German who had headed west to make his fortune, only to find himself running a seedy hotel in a two-bit trail town in the Oregon wilderness. He was a scarecrow of a man, very proper and businesslike—and about as steady as a leaf in a windstorm. Winslow could understand why the madam gained such small comfort from his assurances.

Winslow found himself studying Kate Harrow. She was a tall, striking woman with a wide face and dark emerald eyes set well apart under impressive brows. She had kept her figure despite her age, which he figured to be close on to forty. She was not dressed flashily, but her clothing was expensive, with a taste he had not seen since he quit the more populous centers of the sprawling continent years ago.

But hell, she was, after all, a madam. And those three girls she was so anxious to protect were whores in her employ. Pretty whores, to be sure, but soiled doves nevertheless.

"What did you expect, Kate?" he asked her abruptly. "This is as good a town as any other, and the men in it are just as willing as those in any other. What's wrong with their money?"

"That's not the point."

"Sure it is. You think your girls are too good for the men in this town. Where are you heading, Kate? You found a place on this here continent that deals out only perfumed gentlemen for your perfumed whores?"

Kate straightened, her face flushing. For a moment it looked as if he had struck her. And for a moment he wished he had not spoken as bluntly as he had. He reached out to place his hand over hers, to calm her down while he managed an apology of sorts. But she pulled her hand away, her emerald eyes flashing.

"I guess I made a mistake about you," she said bitterly. "I should have known better. And now, I suppose, you'll be comin' up to the second floor later to collect your reward."

"That isn't so, Kate. And I guess I did speak out of turn. If so, I'm sorry. But sometimes I get tired of the pretensions of others. I guess I should get just as tired of my own."

She looked at him for a long moment, and he could feel her anger subsiding as she studied his face. Then she sighed and pulled her glass of beer closer.

"I suppose I shouldn't be so touchy. You're only being honest. What you say has more than a bit of truth to it." She laughed bitterly. "Where am I going, you ask? Seattle.

There, in that mean little logging camp on the coast, I hope to begin anew. But there'll be no perfumed gentlemen, I assure you.''

"No, there won't, Kate."

"But I have journeyed there already and bought a house. It's a good one, and I have been promised that my girls and I will be left alone to follow our profession in peace.'' She paused and looked at him closely, as if it were very important to her that he understand. "You see, wherever my girls and I find ourselves successful, the politicians and the other big men of the community move in for their piece of the pie. It happened in St. Louis. It happened in Denver.''

"But you don't think it will happen in Seattle.''

"No."

"You're a fool, Kate."

She smiled wanly and nodded. "I suppose so. But I have sunk everything in renting a stage and buying the house waiting for us. I can't turn back now.''

"Who's going to drive your stage now that you've fired that drunk?''

She sighed. "The driver came to me a few hours ago and promised me that he'll be sober for the rest of the journey. And I'll see to it that he has no more spirits hidden on the stage.''

"And you believe him?''

"What choice do I have?''

Winslow shrugged his powerful shoulders and sipped his beer. "None, I suppose.''

"Will you help me, Scott? Tonight, I mean.''

"What do you want me to do?''

"If you could just keep watch on the second floor where the girls are sleeping. I am sure that once it got around that you were on guard, there would be no further trouble.''

"And what are you offering in payment?"

She sighed and leaned back. "If that is your price, then I suppose I have no choice but to grant it. Still, you disappoint me. I had thought you were different."

"I'm a man, Kate—no different from any of the others who walk upon this planet. I have better table manners than some, and I don't usually drink myself into a stupor—though I must admit there have been times when such a course appealed to me. I try to be no meaner than I have to be to survive, but I have my hungers too, Kate. Of all women, you should know better than to trust any man or think that any one of us is different."

"Which girl would you want?"

He smiled and leaned back in his chair. "It has been a long time for me, Kate. And it will be a hell of a lot longer before I purchase a woman, under any conditions. Call it pride, if you will. Foolish pride. But there you are. You get my services free, just for the asking."

"Then why . . . ?"

"I just wanted to know if you were prepared to pay your way—like the rest of us."

She frowned and looked more closely at him, as if she were seeing him for the first time. "You are a strange man, Scott."

"How so, Kate?"

"I don't know, really. But you seem out of place here, so far from civilization."

Winslow laughed. "Civilization? Is that what you call it?" He finished his beer and stood up. "All right, Kate. Let's go back to the hotel and see what we can do to keep those blushing beauties of yours out of the arms of the uncouth men of Baker."

Without comment, Kate left her beer and stood up. The saloon went silent again as the two started across the room.

They were passing close by the end of the bar when Lester Terman slapped his whiskey glass down sharply on the bar and chuckled. "That's the way, Winslow," he said. "The clap'll make a man of you."

Winslow saw Kate's face grow pale. But she said nothing as she continued on past the bar. Winslow did not keep going, however. He swung around, grabbed Terman's shoulder, and dragged him away from the bar. Frantic, Terman tried to duck as Winslow swung a roundhouse that caught him flush on the tip of his chin. There was a sickening crack as Terman's jaw broke under the impact. His hand clutching his shattered jaw, Terman slammed back against the bar, then slid to the floor. Groaning, he rolled over onto a brass spittoon, overturning it. Tears of pain filled his eyes as he looked up at the faces of those staring down at him. But not a single man reached down to help him.

Winslow turned away and strode from the saloon with Kate. As they crossed the street together, she shuddered. "That awful man," she muttered.

"And me," Winslow said, catching something in her voice. "That awful Scott Winslow, as well. Isn't that what you are thinking?"

She glanced at him, surprised at his quickness. "Why, yes, but . . . ."

"I didn't give him much of a chance to defend himself, right?"

"Yes. I suppose that's it."

"You see? As I told you, I'm no better than the worst scoundrel here. Don't ever forget that."

"I'm sorry. I didn't mean to imply that. But you did ask."

"Forget it. I understand how you feel. If it makes any sense to you, I feel the same way myself. But that fellow

21

and I have had our run-ins before. And at any rate, one thing for sure was accomplished.''

"What's that?" she asked as they entered the hotel lobby.

"Once the word gets around that I'm sleeping on a mattress upstairs in the hall, there won't be too many foolish enough to try me. In a way, what I did back there was kind of an advertisement."

She shuddered. "Yes. I suppose it was, at that."

As she preceded Winslow up the stairs, he shook his head. It was strange, but not too long before he had been sure that all the fires within him had been burned out. Now here he was doing what he could to save a madam and her three working girls from being molested. It was a hell of a screwy way to find out that the fires were still burning—that he still was very much alive, after all.

The wagon train was bedded down for the night. Behind his own wagon, Paul Smathers had just finished dousing his fire and was getting ready to retire for the night. At thirty-two, Smathers—Deacon Smathers as he was called—was a wiry rake of a man. Despite the sun and the wind and the foul weather that had dogged their journey through the Rockies, the deacon's face remained untouched, a sickly milk white. His eyes, peering out from behind owlish wire spectacles, were a pale, washed-out blue. His lips were thin, passionless. A nervous, unhappy man, his most noticeable characteristic was the habit he had of plucking at his stringy neck with his long, pale fingers, as if he felt some invisible hand closing around it.

The trek through the mountains to this town had been a long one, and Smathers was grateful for the brief respite Baker offered. He had just finished making the rounds of the wagon train, carefully avoiding Candy Walsh's wagon, and had done what he could to comfort the settlers. Though they had a final set of mountains to traverse before reaching the promised Willamette Valley and though they had heard rumors of hostile Indian activity in the area, God would see them through. God and the U.S. cavalry. Smathers had arranged for an escort through the Blue Mountains when they had passed the fort twenty-five miles down the trail, and the soldiers were due to meet them in Baker in the next day or two. And despite the increasing chill in the air, the army assured them they would be across the mountains in plenty of time—well before the snows closed them in.

Now, with everyone asleep, with the campfires dying and the stars gleaming overhead, Deacon Smathers had only the fierce ache in his heart to contend with—the agonizing fire that simply would not die.

Impulsively, Smathers fell to his knees and clasped his hands before him. His face reflecting the dim glow from the stars, his voice a hoarse, barely audible whisper, he called out to his God for help.

"Grant me your Grace, my Lord," he cried. "I am but a poor soul in torment. I know I have sinned. In my heart I have lusted after this woman Candy Walsh—and others too, I know. But I have tried so hard to follow in the path of righteousness for your own sake. Do not abandon me now! Send me a sign that I still enjoy your Grace! I must know! I must have a sign! I have much to do, and there are so many who depend on me!"

Smathers bowed his head, trembling, and clasped his hands even more tightly as he waited for some indication that God did indeed still regard him as one of the chosen few who someday would sit at his side in Paradise. But the sign Smathers craved didn't come, and the deacon continued to tremble—for he knew that his was a jealous God who at any moment and in all his terrible fury might simply open his hand and let Smathers plunge into the flaming pit of everlasting damnation.

So Deacon Smathers waited and prayed for some sign that his call had not gone unheeded. And while he did so, his damnation continued apace, for in his heart he still ached for Candy Walsh, and in his mind's eye he saw her bewitching smile and the awful loveliness of her slim form. He groaned aloud, gave up beseeching his jealous God, and wept.

Moving silently through the night past the line of dark wagons on his way into Baker, Matt Cord glanced over and saw the dim figure of Deacon Smathers as the cleric knelt piously on the ground, his hands clasped in supplication.

Cord snorted softly in derision. The milksop was asking for guidance, was he? Well, he would need more than prayers now. Matt had only contempt for the deacon. From the moment he had first clapped eyes on the divine, he had seen him for what he was—a stripling completely out of his element on this trek.

Matt Cord certainly was in *his* element. His real name was Mort Calisher, but he hadn't used it in so many years that he now answered instinctively to Matt Cord. And now he was back doing what he liked best—leading an unsuspecting wagon train to an unexpected fate.

The next wagon Cord passed belonged to Tim Curry, a rebel who had abandoned the Confederate cause, and Samantha Ridley, that crazy woman Tim had picked up at Fort Boise, Idaho Territory. As Matt Cord neared the wagon, the music from the reb's harmonica filled the damp night with languor. Continuing on down the length of the wagon, Matt caught sight of Curry sitting up on the wagon seat as he played the doleful tune.

In her rocker in front of the wagon, with the campfire

glowing warmly behind, sat the large, rawboned woman Curry had let join him at the fort. Why the young reb had chosen to take this woman with him was a mystery to Matt. There was nothing between them, that was for damn sure. She was like a child at times and was easily old enough to be his mother. But Matt didn't dwell on the incongruity of this odd relationship; he had other, more important matters to think on.

Matt only dimly recognized the melody Curry was playing, but it filled him with a vague sadness that made him uneasy. To be thus moved angered Matt, since it stirred to life emotions and regrets he chose not to contemplate. Passing Samantha Ridley, he glanced at the woman, doing nothing to hide the sullen distaste the reb's mournful tune aroused in him.

As Samantha's crazed eyes met the wagon master's, she stopped rocking. Her face came alive. Suddenly she jumped up and pointed her long, bony finger at Matt.

"They will kill us!" she cried. "The savages! All of us! But you first! Take your knife with you! You must take your knife!"

At once Tim jumped from the wagon seat to calm the woman. Softly, gently, he spoke to her, until at last she settled back down into her rocker. Leaning back in it, she began rocking once more, her eyes shut tightly, a deep and barely audible crooning coming from her.

Apologetically, Tim looked over at the wagon master. "Don't mind her, Matt. This talk of Red Feather and his renegades has upset her, that's all."

"She don't worry me none," Matt told Curry, his voice laced with contempt. "I don't pay no attention to a crazy woman. What I'm wondering is why in hell you do."

Tim looked at Matt for a long moment, then shrugged. "I don't think I would be able to explain that to you."

"Guess you wouldn't, at that," Matt agreed, and continued on.

Noah and Ruth Whittington, the oldest pair in the wagon train, occupied the next wagon. They were sitting in camp chairs beside their fire and had heard everything Samantha had said. Noah, his arm around his wife, nodded solemnly in greeting to Matt as he approached.

Matt didn't bother to respond as he continued past their wagon. He thought of them as a pair of old sparrows sitting on a bare branch in winter. But they never complained, and they always kept their wagon up with the rest, and it was always in line. The only thing they needed, it seemed, was each other, and that kind of devotion Matt Cord found not only incomprehensible, but just a mite unnerving. So Matt had as little to do with the couple as possible.

Phil and Mary Turner were inside the next wagon, bickering again. The newlyweds were too young and inexperienced for this undertaking, and Matt was surprised they had lasted as long as they had. But he was pleased, too, that they had not yet turned back, since they had the best-stocked wagon of the lot. Everything in it was of the finest quality. It would make fine plunder.

"Hey, Matt," Candy Walsh called from the darkness of her wagon as the wagon master walked by. "Where you heading?"

Matt pulled up. As his eyes grew accustomed to the gloom, he saw Candy and Bill Walsh looking out at him through the wagon's back flap. "Think I'll go into Baker and scare up a drink."

"A drink?" Candy asked. "Is that *all* you're looking for?"

Matt laughed. "Not entirely."

"Good luck!" she sang out mischievously. She was about to add something else, but before she could, Bill pulled her abruptly out of sight. Matt heard the sound of their sudden tussle, punctuated by Candy's giggles. He moved on.

Those two were some pair, they were. It hadn't taken Matt long to figure them out or for them to admit he was right. They were on the run from a well-connected politico they had conned in Denver—and were hoping for a new batch of suckers when they reached Seattle. He had done his best to encourage them in that hope. It amused him to do this, knowing as he did that they would never reach Washington Territory.

Matt Cord headed on into Baker, where he hoped to find in the Loggers' Palace not only a cool drink, but also his accomplice, Bim Stagger. For that reason, Matt was just a mite nervous. If Bim wasn't in the saloon, it meant trouble. Finding Red Feather and his band in these mountains without Bim's help would be an almost impossible task.

He reached town and headed down the narrow street toward the Loggers' Palace. It was a poor excuse for a town, with a muddy lane for a street and a chill dampness hanging like a pall over the low huddle of buildings. The only street lights were a couple of coal-oil lamps hanging from posts in front of the hotel and the saloon. Toward this dim light Matt glided, an unkempt scarecrow of a man with hazel eyes and a receding chin.

Entering the saloon, he was relieved to catch sight of Bim Stagger almost at once. The big fellow was sitting at a table in the farthest corner, a glass of beer clutched in his huge paw. The logger moved his head almost imperceptibly, and Matt drifted over to the bar and ordered a beer, then took it casually over to the table. Bim's right eye was swollen and there was an ugly, purple bruise covering his right cheekbone.

"What the hell happened to you?" Matt inquired as

27

he settled into his chair. "You look like you got hit by a falling tree."

"I got taken down a peg, that's for sure," Bim admitted. "There's some whores stayin' at the hotel across the street. They're on their way to Seattle, so I hear. I took a fancy to one of them—a real pretty little thing—and got my head rung."

"You mean she did that to you?"

"Naw. Feller named Scott—the gambler who works this saloon here. He had other ideas."

"Bigger than you, is he?"

"No, but maybe smarter."

"Where is he now?"

Bim chuckled. "Where do you think?"

Matt smiled wryly at Bim, then frowned as a thought occurred to him. "You say them girls are headin' for Seattle. How they travelin'?"

"The madam has her own stage and driver."

Matt smirked, wondering if this was something he should consider. But after a moment he concluded that involving the stage in his plans would only confuse matters—it was the wagon train he was after. Matt sipped his beer and shrugged. First things first, he told himself.

"Okay," he said to Bim, "what can you tell me? Where's Red Feather?"

"He's waitin' to palaver with you at Deadman's Pass Station. You know where that is?"

Matt nodded. He knew the place—had used it himself on occasion. It was an abandoned way station high in the Blue Mountains and just south of Deadman's Pass. The stage line that had built it had gone bankrupt when the Indian trouble broke out. There were corrals and at least one log building that was in pretty good shape. Even though the station was well hidden from the main trail, Matt would have little difficulty finding it.

28

"Unfortunately the wagon train arranged for a cavalry escort at that fort on the Burnt River," Matt said. "If it shows up, I'll have to let Red Feather know."

Bim leaned forward, his battered face twisting into a grin. "That don't hardly seem likely. Just this morning some soldier boys were pulled out of Baker back to the fort. It seems the cavalry is pulling out. They're needed farther south—all the way to Texas, I hear. Somethin' about the Comanche raising hell down there. Seems them bastards are taking advantage of the war back east to return to their old hunting grounds. They've been roaming at will all through Texas and right on down into Mexico."

Matt leaned back in his chair. This was good news—so good he found it difficult to believe. "You sure they ain't going to detail a small contingent to ride with them wagons anyway—at least as far as the pass?"

Bim shrugged. "I don't know. You'll just have to wait and see. But it sure as hell don't look like it. Those soldier boys said the Burnt River fort is being closed up till things simmer down and Fort Boise is back to full strength."

Matt took a deep breath. He hated to believe it, but everything was going beautifully—just like the last time. As before, this wagon train had no real leader. Though the deacon had so anointed himself, he was a duck out of water, and few paid any attention to him. Furthermore, Smathers was a Calvinist, and the only other members of the wagon train of that persuasion were Amanda and Joshua Beechwood. So weak a leader was the deacon that he had offered little resistance when Matt joined up and then took over as wagon master. Hell, the four-eyed milksop was even grateful to him, as were most of the others.

"How're things goin'?" Bim asked. "Them pilgrims discovered what a lousy wagon master you are?"

Matt chuckled. "By the time they do, it'll be too late."

"Just make sure that half-breed gets what he wants, Matt. I have to log in those mountains, don't forget. And I don't like the way that red devil looks at me sometimes."

"Don't worry. He'll get enough to satisfy even him." Then, glancing around the saloon, Matt asked, "If those soiled doves across the street ain't available, what's this town got to offer?"

Bim shrugged. "You interested in some squaws I got stashed away at my camp outside of town?"

"Squaws?"

"Flatheads. Pretty as pear blossoms and just as sweet. And they got no word for no. Not to a white man, anyway."

Matt felt his loins stirring. "How far?"

"Couple of miles."

"You got horses?"

Bim grinned. "All saddled. And there's plenty of booze in the saddlebags."

Matt finished his beer and stood up. "Let's go, mountain man. Just so long as I get back in time to make sure that cavalry is not coming along."

"Don't fret," Bim said as he led the way out of the saloon. "We'll be back in plenty of time." He grinned lopsidedly at Matt. "And about ten pounds lighter."

Exploding in laughter, the two men moved out onto the street toward the livery.

The braying laughter carried across the street and through the open window of Kate Harrow's hotel room. Still awake, she was sitting by the window, looking down at the dark street and at the two men leaving the saloon. She had wrapped a black woolen shawl over her shoulders. Nevertheless, as she watched the two figures move off down the street, a chill fell over her. That sudden, harsh outburst of laughter was a familiar sound to her—all too familiar. It was the cruel, unmistakable bark of male animals on the prowl and reminded her of the baying of wolves or the yipping call of the coyote—cries in the night that had been sending shivers up her spine and those of her girls in every dusty town west of Denver.

She relaxed finally as the two men disappeared into the darkness. If it were not for that gambler on guard in the hallway outside her door, those two might have crossed the street and entered the hotel, filling it with their cruel, insolent laughter—and with their harsh, violent lust.

But once again she had been able to protect her girls. For another night they were safe, and that was all that mattered. Yes, they were the playthings of men. That was their life. But she always had managed to see to it that the men to whom she gave them were at least clean and well mannered—clients, in short, who had more than a passing acquaintance with civilized behavior. For her part, she had always made certain her girls were well versed in all the amenities, never drank to excess, and spoke as ladies should.

But wasn't she a fool to try this hard to protect them? They were, after all, precisely what everyone called them: whores. And Kate was no better than they. Yet this didn't seem to matter. She would be unable to live with herself if she didn't do all in her power to prevent their profession from destroying them, even though she knew in her heart that it already had gone a long way toward doing just that.

She sighed, got up from her chair, and went to the door. Pulling it open softly, she glanced out. Yes, Scott was still out there, asleep on the mattress with his hand under the pillow. In that hand, she knew, he held a loaded revolver. The blanket he had thrown over his shoulders had fallen away. Swiftly she headed down the hall, pulled the blanket up over the man's shoulders, then silently fled back into her room.

31

Shutting the door firmly behind her, Kate undressed and slipped under the covers. She closed her eyes and found herself thinking of that big, strangely bitter man sleeping in the hallway outside her door. Her thoughts of him turned to dreams as she drifted off to sleep.

Chapter 3

Winslow didn't sleep too well on guard and was in the hotel restaurant early the next morning, downing his third cup of coffee, when Kate entered with Captain Daniel Fogarty. This was the first time in more than a month that the cavalry officer had ventured into Baker, and Winslow was glad to see him.

Winslow got to his feet, shook hands with the captain, and invited him and Kate to sit down. A waitress hurried over, and the captain ordered a cup of coffee. Kate ordered nothing. It was obvious that she had another problem that needed solving—she and the captain, that is.

"What's up, Captain?" Winslow inquired, leaning back in his chair. "You didn't come all this way to have breakfast with me and Miss Kate, did you?"

"It's Miss Harrow that's brought me to your table, Winslow," the captain responded solemnly. "I've just come from speaking with those settlers outside of town. I was on my way back to the fort when I saw the stage outside the livery and learned about Miss Harrow here and her girls."

"He doesn't want us to go over the mountains, Scott," Kate said, obviously distressed.

"Indian trouble, Winslow," Fogarty said by way of explanation. "Last spring, before you took root here, we lost an entire wagon train to that renegade Indian you've been hearing about."

"Red Feather?"

The captain nodded grimly. "We've been on his trail all summer, and it looks like he's back in the Blue Mountains. But we haven't had much luck when it comes to nailing him."

"And my guess is you never will. I heard about that wagon train. Pretty grim business, that."

The captain nodded. "The only survivor was a big mountain man, Bim Stagger. I heard you've already met him."

Winslow nodded. "So has Miss Kate."

"Then you can understand how Bim was able to fight his way free. Bim's big enough to get through anything, but I wouldn't want to bet on Matt Cord's chances of getting this wagon train past Red Feather's band of renegades—if that half-breed's back in those mountains."

Winslow leaned forward, his mind suddenly alert. "This Matt Cord—he's the wagon master?"

"That's right."

Winslow let the name sink in. The highwayman who had killed his father was calling himself Matt Cord. "Go on, Captain."

Shaking his head wearily, the captain leaned back in his seat. "When that wagon train passed through our fort a few days ago, we promised the preacher who's leading them that we would send an escort over the mountains with them. But now we can't do it, and that's why I'm here. There's more Indian trouble in Texas, and we just got orders from Fort Boise to head south and back up the

Rangers. I advised the settlers to hold off until spring—and Miss Harrow, too.''

"But we can't wait here all winter, Captain," Kate insisted. "It is out of the question."

The captain nodded grimly. "That's about what the preacher said, too, ma'am."

Both of them looked at Winslow, who leisurely sipped his coffee. They obviously were expecting him to offer some kind of solution. He had no idea what they had in mind, but whatever it was, he was bracing himself to refuse. He had other business—now that he had decided what he must do about the train's wagon master.

The captain cleared his throat. "As I said, Winslow, the preacher is bound and determined to push on over the mountains before winter sets in. I was hoping that perhaps you might prevail upon ten or fifteen of the townsmen to form a mounted escort for the pilgrims."

Winslow smiled ironically at the captain. "And that's not all you had in mind, is it?"

Grudgingly, Fogarty agreed. "I was hoping you might consider leading the escort as well."

"If you would do that, Scott," Kate said, "perhaps my stage could join up with the wagon train."

The captain looked with sudden surprise at Kate.

She answered his unspoken question with a brisk nod. "That's right, Captain. You heard right. You say I shouldn't try to make it over the mountains alone. All right, then—I won't go alone. I'll join up with the settlers."

"You sure they'd go for that, Miss Harrow?" the captain queried, his face flaming in sudden embarrassment at what his words were implying.

"They would," Kate said, turning to face Winslow, "if someone with guts put the prospect squarely to them. If they're Christians, how are they going to turn us down?"

"There's Christians and there's Christians," Winslow

observed coolly. "Depends on how rabid that preacher and his followers are, I suppose. But they aren't going to like having a madam and her girls join their train, and that's for damn sure."

"Well, Winslow," the captain prompted impatiently, "will you recruit an escort? My commanding officer is willing to help provision such a force."

"I'll bet he is," Winslow answered. "Anything to get him off the hook. Hell, Captain, what makes you think these townsmen are any more eager than your troopers to lead a band of fool pilgrims over the mountains?"

"You know damn well our men are willing," the captain replied testily. "That's not the problem. We simply have no choice. I told you—we've got Comanche trouble in Texas."

"By the time your men get there, the Comanche will be in Mexico."

The captain stiffened. "We have our orders, Winslow."

"Sure you do, Captain. And so do the Devil's cohorts. But you'll not get me to mix with this foolishness." Winslow stood up. "You'll have to find someone else to pull the U.S. cavalry's chestnuts out of the fire. I have other business."

Winslow saw the sudden disappointment on Kate Harrow's face, but he didn't allow it to sway him. It was about time for him to finish what he had started three years ago.

Winslow hurried up the hotel stairs to his room. Once inside, he checked out his Sharps carbine, then lifted his six-gun from the holster hanging on the bedpost. He carried a derringer while gambling—a double-barreled .41— but for what he had in mind now he needed his Colt.

Swinging the Colt out over his bed, Winslow emptied the cylinder on the sheets. Then he dry-fired it a few times to test the action and checked the firing pin to make sure it was clean of any gummy deposits. Then he reloaded. Satisfied, he replaced the Colt in the holster and strapped the gunbelt around his waist. Picking up his Sharps, Winslow left the room and hurried from the hotel, heading out of town to the field where the wagon train had made its camp the evening before.

His plan was deceptively simple. He had no intention of killing the man who now called himself Matt Cord. Instead, Winslow would take him prisoner and return him to Fort Yuma, where he would be forced to serve out his sentence. Death would be too easy a way out for his father's killer. And Winslow no longer felt that bitter, congealing need for a killing vengeance—only a sudden, deep longing to end this miserable business once and for all.

He reached the campground and began to move swiftly but casually among the wagons and campfires, searching for the wagon master. He was careful to keep his expression easy and to nod in a friendly fashion whenever anyone caught his eye. But his patience soon wore thin. Though he had covered the entire campground and checked all six wagons, he had found no trace of Matt Cord. Finally he wandered toward the small crowd that was gathered around a thin fellow dressed in black. This, he realized, must be the preacher that Captain Fogarty had said was leading the settlers. Though Winslow had not wanted to inquire openly about the wagon master's whereabouts, he now realized he had no alternative. If anyone would know where Cord was, the preacher would.

The cleric was backed up against his wagon, arguing with some animation with a bearded man and his wife. Other settlers were listening intently as they crowded close, occasionally throwing in a few choice remarks of their own. Before Winslow reached the group, he caught sight of Kate Harrow standing off to one side. Immediately Winslow understood why the discussion was so hot and heavy. Kate already must have asked the preacher's permission to join her stagecoach to the wagon train. As Fogarty had predicted earlier, the preacher and his pilgrims were not all that eager for such an arrangement.

Realizing he would have to bide his time before asking about Cord, Winslow drifted over to where Kate was standing. He was drawn to her, he suddenly realized, because she seemed so defiantly and courageously alone.

"I see you are a very stubborn woman," he remarked.

Compressing her lips firmly, the woman nodded. She obviously was still upset with him for refusing to recruit an escort for the wagon train.

Winslow turned his attention to the heated discussion. A few angry words came to him clearly. He winced and glanced at Kate. "I hope you have tin ears as well."

Kate sighed, her eyes bleak. "I have heard worse, Scott. And besides, I always have a consolation."

"And what might that be?"

"Sooner or later, these pious hypocrites end up in my parlor."

Winslow chuckled and looked back at the debating settlers. The one standing beside the preacher—a bearded, handsome man in his early forties—was the same fellow whose lead wagon Winslow had seen plunging through town the evening before.

"Any idea who that bearded gent standing beside the preacher is?" he asked Kate.

"Yes. He was the first one I spoke to. Name's Beechwood. He saw no reason why I couldn't join the wagon train. He seemed pleasant enough. But it was his wife who put a stop to such talk and called the preacher. That's why we've got this debate. She's that gaunt, pinched woman at his side—would have none of it. He called her Amanda, and she's a cold, unloving woman, I'm thinking.''

The preacher was holding forth now. He was anxious to warn his pilgrims what the Bible had to say about such matters. But suddenly one of the settlers standing with a well-endowed young blond asked if they were going to stay there and argue all day. He demanded a vote be taken at once. It was obvious the deacon didn't have the hold of a shepherd on his flock.

A young fellow wearing a battered rebel cap sang out then. He insisted that they had no choice but to take Kate and her girls along with them. After all, it was the Christian thing for them to do, wasn't it? At once an elderly couple joined their voices to his. The fellow who had just demanded they vote glanced over at the young Johnny Reb and made a ribald crack concerning his motives, a nasty grin splitting his unshaven face as he did so. At once the young man took an angry stride toward the older man.

Cooler heads prevailed, and sensing the danger of any further discussion, the deacon called for a vote. All those who were against letting Kate's stagecoach join the wagon train were to raise their hands. The result was five against and five in favor of the plan.

At that point, Winslow decided to kill two birds with one stone.

"Where's the wagon master?" he called out. "Bring him out here and let him cast the deciding vote!"

The deacon frowned, and the rest of the settlers turned in surprise to face Winslow. "Just what's your interest in this business, mister?" the unshaven fellow inquired, not very politely.

"Never mind that. Where's the wagon master?"

"He's not in camp," the preacher announced. "After meeting with Captain Fogarty, he left to scout the mountain pass. I don't expect to see him until we reach the Grande Ronde River.''

"In that case," Winslow said, "I guess I'll be joining this here wagon train. My name's Scott Winslow. The captain asked me to do what I could to help you settlers get through the mountains—and that's just what I aim to do.''

"Why, that's . . . fine," the preacher responded uncertainly. "The captain did say he was going to try rounding up some townsmen to help us through the pass. How many men are joining the escort party?''

"Just me so far. But I aim to see if anyone else has the spine for it. I doubt it, though. Isn't a man among these here townsmen who'd be worth a damn in Indian country. They know it and I know it. But that doesn't mean I can't help some. I know this country.''

"We are much obliged, sir," the preacher said.

"Good. Then may I presume I will be able to take part in your councils?''

"Of course.''

"And vote along with the rest of you?''

"Certainly.''

"In that case, since your wagon master's missing, permit me to break this here deadlock. I believe in safety in numbers, so I vote to allow Miss Kate and her stagecoach to join the wagon train. And since her driver has proven somewhat unreliable, I'm volunteering to drive her coach. Will that suit you, preacher?''

The preacher didn't have it in him to protest any longer. With a fatalistic shrug, he said, "As you wish, Mr. Winslow. And can I count on it that this madam and her . . . girls will be your responsibility as well?''

"You can.''

As the crowd around the preacher broke up, Kate looked quizzically at Winslow. "You are a strange man,

Scott—and just a bit presumptuous. I told you last night I hired back my driver. Do you fancy yourself as good a man as he?''

"Better. You needn't worry about my ability to handle that team of yours. I had an excellent teacher."

Tipping his hat to her, Winslow strode off.

Watching him go, Kate frowned thoughtfully. She liked the man well enough and was grateful for what he had just done, but there obviously was much more to him than met the eye—and just what that might be caused a warning voice to sound deep within her.

Matt Cord didn't spare his broad-chested gray horse, and by noon of his second day on the trail, he was sixty-five miles out of Baker, high in the Blue Mountains, topping a ridge that overlooked the abandoned Deadman's Pass Station. He reined in impatiently, then leaned forward in his saddle, viewing the abandoned way station less than half a mile below him, which Red Feather was using as his headquarters.

As Matt studied the buildings, he couldn't deny the pleasurable anticipation he felt. His prospects were good, especially now that he knew for sure there would be no cavalry escort for the wagon train. This news would be welcome indeed to Red Feather, and as the bearer of such tidings, Matt expected a fine greeting indeed from the renegade.

Woodsmoke was coiling almost straight up from the chimney of the main building, and Matt could see a few of Red Feather's band moving around the compound. They didn't seem to be taking any precautions, and this surprised Matt. Red Feather was a very efficient and very careful marauder, whom Matt had come to respect mightily since that attack they had collaborated on the spring before. He wasn't usually this careless.

Cord sat back in his saddle and was about to urge his mount off the ridge when he heard the faint whinny of a horse behind him. Swinging around in his saddle, he saw four Indians astride their horses within ten feet of him. Each one had a repeating rifle in his right hand—and each muzzle was staring with deadly intent at Matt's head.

An almost disabling knife-edge of fear slid into his gut. Swallowing carefully so as not to reveal his terror, he held up his right hand, palm out, in the traditional sign of peace.

"I am Cord, Red Feather's friend," he told them. "I have ridden far to see him, for I bring him good news!"

One of the Indians silently urged his mount closer, the muzzle of his rifle remaining fixed on Matt's face. When he was close enough, the Indian leaned over and pulled Matt's rifle from its scabbard, tossed it to an Indian behind him, then relieved Matt of his six-gun as well. This he stuck in his waistband, a look of cold disdain on his face as he sat back in his saddle.

"I know you," the Indian said. "You are Crooked Face, the white man who betrays his own kind. You have come to lead more of your people into our trap." His stone face became even colder. "Is that not so, Crooked Face?"

Matt didn't much like the sound of that, but all he could do was nod grudgingly.

"Come," the Indian said. "We will take you to Red Feather."

The Indian put his horse ahead of Matt's and led the way down the slope toward the way station, the rest of the Indians following close behind. Matt was simmering and a little alarmed at this greeting. Surely Red Feather had expected him. Why then had he sent such an insulting brave to greet him? The half-breed renegade was a hard one for Matt to figure.

A Bannock war party had captured Red Feather's

white mother and traded her to a Shoshone chief, who fathered the half-breed. When the boy was ten years old, he and his mother were taken from the Shoshone as one of the conditions of a treaty that both the army and the tribe wished to conclude.

Red Feather's mother died soon after, and he was raised by an exceedingly cruel white couple who had lost their own son to an Indian war party years before. They took every opportunity to verbally and physically abuse the boy, as if he were to blame for their own son's plight. And when Red Feather at age fifteen grew too large and began to fight back, they shipped him off to a boarding school in Salt Lake City. The young Indian rebelled against the rigid life at the school and ran away—back to his Shoshone people.

When Red Feather returned to his tribe, he found that his aged father had been murdered by a troop of drunken cavalry, who had taken it upon themselves one Sunday afternoon to rid the world of all heathens. Beside a small valley stream, the horse soldiers had found only a few lodges, empty of all but women, old men, and children too young to ride. And upon these sad victims the troopers had satisfied their blood lust.

For two weeks Red Feather wandered alone in the vastness of the Blue Mountains, mourning the loss of his father and his people. Then he sought out his white foster parents, arriving at their home on the day of his sixteenth birthday. He celebrated the event by hanging the couple from the rafters in their living room. Around their foreheads he wound a cloth band, and in each band he stuck a red feather.

Now a member of no tribe, Red Feather led a collection of renegades and cutthroats recruited from the Bannock, the Gosiute, and other Shoshone tribes in the area. As their leader he was a law unto himself, striking when and where he wanted, then pulling his troops back and disappearing into the thickly forested mountains of the region. Allied with no chief, he declared that any Indian who did business with the white men and suffered them upon their land was a white man himself. The true Indian, he insisted, would join Red Feather in the mountains, where they would live only to kill whites and avenge the blood of their loved ones.

Matt Cord had almost reached the way station when a filthy, crazed captive of the Indians—Thomas Grant—came screaming from a clump of pines toward the approaching horses. Matt pulled up in confusion. Grant had chains around his neck and ankles, but he managed, nevertheless, to hobble with considerable speed straight for Matt.

"You Judas!" the apparition cried, his eyes wide with madness. "Judas! I'll kill you!"

He reached up and grabbed hold of Matt's boot. His grip was astonishingly strong, and as the Indians laughed at Matt's discomfiture, Grant began to tug furiously on his leg in a frenzied attempt to drag him from his saddle.

Matt reached down and grabbed the chain around the madman's neck. Twisting it cruelly, he dragged Grant backward. With a strangled cry, the man released his hold on the boot, and at once Matt lashed out with his foot, catching Grant in the face and sending him spinning to the ground, blood exploding from both nostrils.

As an aged squaw came running to tend to the prisoner, Matt spurred his horse on through the yelping ring of Indians. He saw Red Feather standing in front of the station's main building and turned his horse toward him, his Indian escort trailing behind, still sounding their pleasure at Matt's encounter with Grant.

As Matt rode closer to Red Feather, he was reminded once again that the only thing that testified to the Indian's white blood was his taller stature and icy blue eyes. Everything else about this fierce warrior was pure Shoshone.

Matt pulled up and dismounted. Red Feather did not greet him with any speech of welcome, but simply let his cold stare flick over the man a moment before turning and leading him into the building. Matt followed, unable to shake the chill fear that fell over him as he entered the darkened, damp-smelling building. He cleared his throat as the Indian pointed to a chair beside a rotting kitchen table.

"How long you goin' to keep that lunatic, Red Feather?" he complained, taking a seat by the table. "He's gettin' pretty damn wild. Near pulled me off my horse back there."

Red Feather sat down and regarded Matt closely for a moment. Then he said, in almost perfect English, "I have given him to a squaw who lost her brave to a white man's bullet. He carries water for her and brings kindling to her lodge. At times he is quite content, though he continues to rave. He speaks often of you—and the way you led his family and the rest of those settlers into my trap." For a moment a bleak smile lit Red Feather's face. "I think it is good for my men to look upon him and realize that this pitiful, soulless creature is a white man."

Matt shuddered, despite himself. "Your men have taken my weapons," he said with some indignation. "There's no need for that. I come as a friend."

A young squaw brought a steaming coffeepot over and filled two tin cups on the table in front of them. Both men pulled their coffee toward them. As Red Feather sipped his scalding brew, his eyes caught and fixed Matt with a chilling and malevolent stare. Matt's last statement had evidently incensed him, but he was doing what he could to control his anger.

"No white man is a friend to Red Feather," the Indian said evenly, with measured scorn. "I use you, Matt Cord, because you also have no soul and will betray your own kind. I detest you. All my men detest you, as well. They call you Crooked Face. But you are useful to us. You help us kill your own kind, and for that reason we let you live—though we feel unclean when we are near you and know that it will take strong medicine to wash out the stain on our souls that comes from letting your shadow cross ours.''

Red Feather's words, spoken softly and carefully, sent more than a shiver up Matt's backbone. With a shaking hand, he reached for his own cup of coffee.

"Hell,'' Matt protested feebly, attempting a smile. "That ain't no way to talk to an old friend, Red Feather. I come bearing great news. The cavalry is pulling out. The wagon train I'm bringing you won't have no escort.''

Red Feather smiled. "You think I did not know this?''

"Well, it's the first I heard.''

"The horse soldiers are making much noise as they move out of the fort—we can hear them all the way up here.'' His smile hardened and he leaned closer, his eyes glinting. "Now, when will your wagon train be passing through our Deadman's Pass?''

"One week. Two on the outside. The river might give us trouble, but I don't think so.''

"Do not delay. Signs of an early winter are everywhere. First come the rains and then the snow.''

"We'll be there.''

"And so will we.'' Red Feather put down his coffee and leaned back in his chair. "You will want only the money and gold, as before?''

"Sure. That's the way we handled it the last time, ain't it?''

Red Feather regarded Matt with a mixture of scorn and appreciation. "And my people can drink deep of the blood of the white man and take what other plunder we wish—as before?''

''Suits me.''

''Yes,'' Red Feather said, ''of course it does. I learned much while I lived with the white man, but I was never able to fathom the duplicity of men such as yourself. Outlaws—yes, that is the word for your kind. You exist in a land that is outside the law, outside compassion or feelings of any kind. Tell me, do you not hate these people you lead into my hands?''

''Hell, no. This is just business for me, Red Feather. I don't hate them. Why the hell should I?''

Red Feather nodded. ''Just so. And that is the wonder of it. It would be a curious and a terrible thing to peer into your soul. Or perhaps not. Perhaps if I could look into that abyss, I would see . . . nothing.''

''Hey, now, Red Feather,'' Matt protested. ''There ain't no call for you to talk like that. Besides, I don't hardly know what you're saying. So let's stick to business. We got a deal and that's all that matters.''

Red Feather nodded. ''Yes, Crooked Face, we have a deal.''

Matt finished the foul coffee, stood up, and stuck out his hand to Red Feather. With visible distaste, the half-breed took Matt's hand and shook it.

''Leave now,'' he told Matt. ''There are many in this camp who are not happy to see you—your presence makes them uneasy. It would be wise for you to ride out soon.''

''That don't bother me none,'' Matt said. ''I been riding for two days, and I have a couple of more days to go. So I'll be moving on.'' He grinned crookedly at Red Feather. ''Thanks for the hospitality.''

Red Feather smiled thinly. ''Do not be sarcastic with me,'' he told him softly.

Matt felt himself go pale at the menace in Red Feather's

voice. Hurrying from the building, he mounted up. When he looked warily around for some sign of that madman Grant, he was relieved to see he was nowhere in sight. The party of braves that had escorted Matt into the station was still mounted up, waiting for him to ride out. They watched him impassively, coldly.

"What about my weapons?" Matt demanded of Red Feather, who appeared in the doorway.

The Indian turned to one of the mounted braves and barked an order in Shoshone. The brave rode closer to Matt and handed back his rifle and six-gun. Hastily plunging the rifle back into its scabbard and holstering his revolver, Matt pulled his horse around and started across the yard, heading southeast toward the Grande Ronde River.

Five minutes later, he glanced back at the way station and saw part of Red Feather's band pulling out, heading into the mountains in the direction of Deadman's Pass.

At the same time, he felt the first, heavy drops of rain and with it a sudden gust of chill wind. Glancing up, he saw banks of dark clouds rolling in over the peaks from the west. *Could Red Feather be right about that early winter?* he wondered as he hastily pulled his slicker out of his saddle roll. He sure as hell hoped not. And then Matt chuckled at his concern. Hell, what difference did an early winter make to him now? Or to the settlers either, for that matter?

Chapter 4

After spending a day purchasing supplies and making needed repairs to their wagons, the settlers pulled out of their Baker campsite at dawn of the same day Matt Cord reached Red Feather's mountain hideaway. Following at a discreet distance was the rented stagecoach carrying Kate Harrow and her girls.

Up in the box, with Dr. Braden Throckmorton beside him, Winslow was surprised at how quickly he once more became accustomed to the feel of horses' reins—or ribbons, as they were called. His father, he realized with a sudden rush of fondness, had taught him well.

The trail the wagon train was following was deeply rutted, and for a while it followed the vagaries of a swift-running mountain stream. On the other side of the trail, a thick stand of pine, dark and impenetrable, shouldered close to the wagons and the passing stage—so close that every now and then branches would scrape against the sides of the coach, forcing the doctor to duck down quickly to avoid being swept off the coach.

Above the rattle of the stage, Winslow caught at

times the call of a goldfinch deep in the pines. Its haunting, echoing cry sent a somber chill through him. Unlike anyone else on this journey, Winslow had an uneasy sense of what might be lying ahead for this wagon train. And it didn't please him—though it didn't surprise him—that during the past day he hadn't been able to convince a single townsman to help escort the stage. Matt Cord's disappearance disturbed Winslow, though he didn't know why. The wagon master hadn't seemed to recognize him in that brief glance the evening he rode into Baker. And yesterday morning, when the settlers agreed to let Kate's stage join them, Deacon Smathers had said Cord was simply scouting the trail ahead, which made sense, Winslow supposed. Still, Winslow was uneasy.

His uneasiness came from knowing Cord better than he knew most other men. Careless, unthinking depravity marked the outlaw. He killed not only without compunction, but without notice. What then was a man like this doing leading a wagon train west? It was a hard, tough business, and riches weren't the reward of such a difficult and dangerous undertaking.

Winslow had talked to the cleric before starting out and learned that the deacon leaned heavily on his wagon master's knowledge of the country and trusted Matt Cord implicitly. So, of course, there was always the possibility that Cord had reformed since escaping from Yuma. He might at last have seen the error of his ways and might now be content to pass the remainder of his days as a wagon scout.

But even as Winslow framed this thought, he knew it to be utterly preposterous. All he had to do to refute such a fanciful notion was remember the cold, dead look in Cord's eyes as they flicked over Winslow the other night. There was absolutely no light in them. They were the eyes of a man completely without pity.

Winslow sighed. As he saw it, his only course was to wait until the wagon master rejoined the train and watch the man closely. Taking him captive and bringing him back to Yuma was out of the question now. He would have to deal with Cord quietly, less spectacularly, and in his own time.

Winslow glanced up at the sky. Black clouds had been rolling in ever since they left Baker, but as yet no rain had fallen. Nevertheless, a brisk wind was sweeping down off the peaks ahead of them. On the box beside Winslow, the good doctor countered the cool wind with a warming bottle of medicinal spirits he kept stashed in his black bag for just such emergencies.

"You are a baleful and somber companion, Mr. Winslow," Throckmorton said suddenly. "Here! Take a swig of this and warm your heart as well as your feet!"

Winslow managed a smile. "No thanks, Doc. You saw what Kate did to that last driver who drank too much."

"The man couldn't hold his liquor! You are of a different stripe, I'll wager."

"Maybe. But for now, Doc, why don't you hold off some? Save that for later—we've got ourselves a long ride through those mountains."

The doctor shrugged. "As you say." He capped the fifth and put it back into his bag, which he then tucked away beneath his feet.

A moment later, the first drops of rain began to fall.

The doctor shuddered and pulled a cape up over his shoulders. He was wearing a black, wide-brimmed hat, and in preparation for the downpour he pulled the brim down to shield his neck.

"Ah," he said, "the gentle rain! 'He maketh the sun to rise on the evil and on the good, and sendeth rain on the just and on the unjust alike.' " Throckmorton glanced

51

sidelong at Winslow. "And by the way, my friend, in which category do you place me—and our precious burden below?"

Smiling at the doctor's grandiloquence, Winslow shook his head. "Never could make up my mind when it came to judging folks in your business, Doc. But it sure seems to me that those girls manage to spread some cheer, at that."

"Well said, sir. Yes, indeed. My daughters of Venus do indeed spread cheer." Throckmorton chuckled. "But unfortunately, they have spread at times other things as well—which, of course, is why I am lucky enough to count myself a member of Kate's entourage."

Winslow grinned. "Now don't go telling me any tales out of school, Doc. That's not fair to our daughters of Venus."

"True, my good man. True. We shouldn't gossip. As a very observant cleric once noted, every man has in his own life sins enough, in his own mind trouble enough, and in his own fortune evils enough—so that curiosity after the failings of others cannot be without envy or an evil mind." With a slightly ironic smile, Throckmorton glanced at Winslow. "And certainly, my dear Winslow, we do not wish to be regarded as envious or evil men."

To that oration, Winslow found he could only agree—his amusement tempered with more than a little admiration. The good Dr. Throckmorton had an impressive gift for gab.

The rain increased, but it wasn't heavy, just an annoyance. And soon the clouds passed over and the sun broke through. The wagons made good time even though they were moving up a steady grade, and Winslow found himself enjoying Dr. Throckmorton's eloquence. Soon the man was quoting Shakespeare at some length, and Winslow allowed the ribbons to rest lightly in his hand as he leaned back and listened.

Inside the stage, Kate rested her chin on her palm and gazed out at the dense stand of pine that almost seemed to lean into the stage's interior as they rode past.

For the longest time she had forced herself not to think of that strange, taciturn, rugged man who was now driving her stage. She didn't like what being near Scott Winslow did to her. She always had been proud of the fact that she no longer was vulnerable to such men—that her profession had effectively and completely prevented any such entanglements. She knew what madness could afflict her if ever her resolve should weaken. She had seen what on occasion it had done to her charges over the years. It always amazed and sickened her when she saw how infatuation clouded their thinking and turned them at last into putty—to be worked over and then discarded by careless and brutal men.

No, she told herself defiantly, she would not allow herself to think of Scott Winslow as anything other than the man she was paying to drive her stage. But that thought led to something else, equally disquieting: Why had Scott changed his mind in that fashion? What on earth made him suddenly so eager to leave Baker and take on the task of driving her stage? She didn't for a moment believe it was because of her. He had another reason, she was almost certain—a purpose dark and hidden. She had caught a glimpse of it in his eyes the moment she thanked him for offering to drive the stage. But what was the reason? Why was he up there now in the box with Throckmorton?

Kate sighed and attempted to think of other things. Of Wally Ditwhiler, for one thing. So weary had this trip made her that she increasingly found herself seriously considering the big bluff man's offer. She had met Wally the first night she was in Seattle looking the town over. He had been a most gallant and attentive guide. In fact, it was he who had pointed out the newly constructed three-story rooming house she eventually purchased. With him at her side, the sale had progressed swiftly and was concluded very much to her advantage.

It was just before she left Seattle to return to Denver that the man had made his offer. Marriage was out of the question, of course. But he needed a woman he could respect and love, and he was willing to pay handsomely for the privilege. At the moment he was building a substantial fortune exploiting the lumber in the region, and he assured her that she would want for nothing. When he had seen her hesitation, he had asked her not to give an answer until she returned. He knew she would want—and need—time to think it over.

And that was just what she had been doing these past weeks during this long, interminable journey. For the first time, it seemed, she was beginning to fully comprehend how chancy and empty her present life was—for her as well as for her girls. But there was a stumbling block: Kate realized she could never love Wally Ditwhiler. Even more important, as with so many men she had come to know over the years, she had long since gone beyond Wally in maturity and intelligence. One of the factors that made her girls and her houses so popular was the fact that all of her girls, as well as Kate herself, were surprisingly well educated. This was due in part to her insistence that her houses must always boast a well-stocked library. With Dr. Throckmorton acting as her unofficial librarian, her store of reading matter had been steadily increasing over the years, both in quality and abundance.

Indeed, it was this library that gave Kate and the girls the strength to endure their situation. That store of books was their island of sanity in a crude, violent world. More than half the trunks in the stage's rear boot were filled with

Kate's precious volumes, and they would be the first items unloaded when they reached Seattle.

At any rate, Kate's reading had educated her far beyond the rude, narrow minds that frequented her establishment, and unfortunately Wally Ditwhiler was no exception. While he escorted her about Seattle, he had given freely of his outrageous and opinionated pronouncements with a blithe unawareness of just how limited and inaccurate they were. Supremely confident, he was almost always completely wrong. Only with great difficulty had she been able to keep the smile on her face as she unhesitatingly agreed to the most ridiculous pronouncements.

But what did she expect? How could she ask for anything better? Ditwhiler appeared to be enough of a gentleman to hold to a bargain—and that really was all she could hope for and all she realistically should want.

And then Kate thought of Scott Winslow.

Directly across from Kate, watching her closely, sat Terry Lambert. She was almost certain whom Kate was thinking of at that moment, and she wondered—with a delicious, titillating anticipation—what would happen to all of Kate's plans if she succumbed to Scott Winslow's charms.

Terry firmly clasped the leather strap as she rocked with the ceaseless, metronomic rhythm of the stage. She was a small, slim girl of twenty-two with an abundance of auburn hair, clear intelligent eyes, and a lovely melodious laugh. Indeed, her laugh was her gift to Kate and the other girls, for in the gloomiest of times it alone seemed capable of dispelling the gray clouds that always hung close to an establishment such as theirs.

But Terry hadn't laughed in many weeks. Indeed, her acceptance of Kate and her profession had taken a sudden nosedive the moment she learned—too late to save

55

herself—of Kate's plan to relocate in Seattle. Though she had decided not to confront her madam openly, she thought Kate was a fool. Kate should have given in to those men in Denver. What did it matter if she had to give them a portion of her income? It was a tax, like any other—a price Kate should have been willing to pay to stay in Denver.

Terry sighed inwardly. There had been so many fine prospects for her in Denver. One elderly gentleman had been perfectly mad about her. He was fabulously wealthy and had promised to set her up in her own apartment and visit her only on weekends. But by the time she had made up her mind to accept the man's offer, he had left Denver. Undismayed, she had settled down to wait for his return— but now here she was, halfway to Seattle!

If only she had known Kate had planned to move farther west! She would have accepted the suitor's offer without hesitation. After all, it would have been a perfect arrangement. During the week, while this fine old gentleman was away, she would have been free to seek out a truly desirable catch.

Kate had taught her well. Terry knew the power she could wield over men who thought that love was simply the desire to fondle and use a woman. They had no sense about such things. But a woman who understood this had immeasurable power. It had been true all through history, as Kate's books made so thoroughly clear. Women who knew this secret often gained immense power. Cleopatra. Du Barry. Josephine. Aspasia, the mistress of Pericles. Hadn't Terry read that Pericles had been forced to stand up before his fellow Athenians and plead that Aspasia not be deported? And hadn't he at that time shed tears, thus sparing her?

None of this was lost on Terry. She knew what an enormous power she had over men and knew how she must use it. Unlike Kate, she wouldn't fritter it away.

After all, Kate was little more than a frustrated mother hen, with her girls playing the parts of daughters. If that was all Kate wanted, then fine. But not Terry—from now on she was going to let Kate know that Terry Lambert had declared her independence.

As Terry went over this in her mind, her face lost its peaceful repose and her eyes, still on Kate, grew cold and calculating.

Watching Terry closely was Melody Tinsdale. She saw the firm resolve harden on Terry's face and thought she knew what the other was thinking. Terry had never hidden from the other girls her unhappiness at being uprooted from Denver. Melody knew she had been making plans in Denver, plans that had been shattered by Kate's sudden decision to leave.

Melody thought she knew what Terry would do in retaliation for this disappointment: She would run away as soon as she could find some man to pay her way back to Denver. And what worried Melody was not Terry's foolish desire to find such a man, but what this would do to Kate. Terry was Kate's favorite—something the other girls took for granted—but soon she was going to make Kate very unhappy. And Melody dreaded that, because she needed Kate to take care of her. Without Kate, Melody would have sunk long ago into a black abyss of self-hatred and despair. Before being taken in by Kate, she had suffered terrible depressions—her wrists still bore the scars of three suicide attempts. These disabling depressions came infrequently now, but when they did, only Kate was capable of pulling her together and giving her hope. Kate was her lifeline.

Melody was a dark-haired, impish girl. At times a moody troublemaker, she was more often than not a quick-witted, exciting delight to be with. But when Melody was bad, she was not only bad but mean as well. When such moods overtook her, she transferred her self-loathing to her male clients, taking a malicious delight in puncturing the ego of whoever was with her at the time. Though she had no trouble attracting men to her crib, there were times when they left her couch baffled and not a little disquieted by this strange, moody girl.

Yet they always came back, lured perhaps by the elusive impishness they found in Melody's haunted eyes— and by something else Melody had never realized until Kate explained it to her. These men sensed Melody's deep unhappiness and wanted desperately to be the force that drove that sadness from her. Their reward would be to hear again her delicious peals of laughter. And they wanted this, Kate assured Melody, almost more than they wanted her to pleasure them. It was a matter of pride for them to be able to tell themselves that they had the power to make this beautiful, unhappy girl laugh again.

It was such comforting and invaluable insights that made Melody appreciate Kate. She was more than a mother to Melody—she was a rock of sanity in an otherwise dark and terrifying world. For this reason if for no other, Melody did not want Kate to be hurt by Terry, and as this resolve hardened within her, she felt that old malicious impishness grow within her as well.

She leaned over and poked Terry on the knee. "What are you up to, Terry?" she demanded. "A penny for your thoughts."

"Is that all?" Terry drawled, pulling up suddenly. She had caught that familiar, dangerous gleam in Melody's eye and was instantly aware that trouble was afoot. And Terry was game. Anything to banish the boredom of this unending journey. "My thoughts are worth a lot more than that."

"Are they now? Who would have thought it?"

"If you're in one of your moods, Melody, I'm your match anytime. Just give me an excuse."

The gleam in Melody's eyes brightened. "I just thought you might like to know that I already know what you're thinking. So I don't need to pay that penny."

"Go ahead then. What was I thinking?"

"That you'll soon find a man to take you away from all this. Even in Seattle."

"That's a damned lie!" Terry cried, her face flaming angrily. She was instantly furious to hear Melody expressing aloud, in front of Kate, a resolution she had hoped to keep hidden from the world.

Collette La Tour was sitting beside Terry. Swiftly she grabbed Terry by the arm to restrain her.

"Please, Terry," Collette pleaded. "Don't mind Melody. So what if she thinks she can read your mind? Let her think it." Collette looked at Melody then. "Go ahead, Melody. Tell me what *I'm* thinking, if you can."

"I can't."

"Why not, may I ask?"

"Because there's nothing in your head for you to think with, silly."

With a cry, Collette reached over and grabbed the front of Melody's dress. She was in the act of dragging her off her seat when Kate intervened. Kate's voice was sharp and imperious, her hostile gaze raking the three of them ruthlessly. Before her cold anger, all three girls shrank away and settled back into their seats.

Collette sank back into a corner and began to brood. For Kate's customers, Collette was the exotic, sought-after French expert. The rest of the girls treated her shabbily as a result. To them, she had no class. They regarded her as beneath them, yet they were no better than she. At least she wasn't afraid to really please a man—in a way that few men could resist.

And please them she did. This, at least, gave her some comfort—but not as much as she craved. She longed to be accepted by the other girls. And as she thought of her isolation, even among her own kind, she began to weep softly to herself.

With a sigh, Kate let the girl cry. It was Collette's answer whenever she felt put upon by the other girls—and to every other crisis, as well. But she did it so well, so softly and with such impeccable manners, that it was almost a comfort to hear her.

Kate looked back out at the dark forest that swept past the lurching stage. Though she saw it, she didn't contemplate its dark vastness. She was pondering instead Melody's accusation—and Terry's swift, red-faced denial, the significance of which was not lost on Kate.

Before long, she was going to face an open revolt from Terry, and Kate had no idea how she would handle it. She loved Terry like a daughter, but knew only too well that a time comes when a mother and daughter must part. But even to think of such an eventuality caused Kate to flinch.

What a cruel joke, and what a fool she must be, to have come to regard as a daughter a girl who, as near as Kate could judge, was the purest whore she had ever known—next to herself.

It was almost sundown when the wagon train halted in a high, lush parkland close by a mountain stream. Deacon Smathers had led the wagon train to this spot on the direction and advice of Matt Cord before he left to scout the mountains, and as a result he once again was impressed by his wagon master's knowledge of this high country. Soon the wagons had formed a protective circle in the middle of which they drove their stock, while the stagecoach, arriving late at the campsite, found a spot close by a stand of pine farther up the stream. Fires were soon lit, and late but nourishing suppers were swiftly prepared.

When the moonless night finally descended upon the encampment and the campfires had become but glowing embers, Smathers began his rounds, greeting his people warmly and enjoying their return salutations. As they bedded down for the night, they seemed as happy as he at the progress they had made, and he detected no fear at all concerning the supposed Indian menace that awaited them in these mountains.

Smathers intended to avoid going past Bill and Candy Walsh's campfire and was turning his footsteps toward Tim Curry's wagon when Candy stepped into view and called out softly to him.

His heart thudding in his breast, Smathers turned around. Candy ran toward him and flung her arms about his chest, momentarily resting her head on his shoulder. "Oh, Deacon Smathers!" she cried, "Isn't all this beautiful? It is God's work, is it not? Such grand mountains and thick forests. I feel like I'm Eve entering a new paradise, I'm so excited. And you brought us here like Kit Carson and all those other pathfinders! Aren't you proud?"

"To God goes the glory," Smathers stammered, taken aback by this sudden, gushing outpouring of sentiment.

Blushing, Candy stepped back. "Oh my," she said, her fingers flying up to her mouth. "I am afraid I got carried away, Deacon Smathers. I declare, you must think me a terrible hussy to go running into your arms with such abandon! You must forgive me. It's just that I'm so delighted, so excited by this vision of God's country!"

"It . . . it is impressive, I must admit," Smathers managed, unwilling to step away from Candy's intoxicating presence. He felt himself drowning in her wide eyes, the curve of her lips, the shape of her brow. His head reeled, almost as if he had had too much to drink—an indiscretion he had committed only once in his short, pious life. But he was drunk now, he realized. And dazzled as well.

"Deacon," Candy whispered, stepping suddenly closer. "There's something I must tell you." She moved her body so close to his that when she inhaled they touched.

Groaning inwardly at the heat of her body and the answering passion that flamed from his loins, he nodded quickly. "What is it, Mrs. Walsh? Is there anything wrong?"

"Deacon, I must confess something to you that has burned at my soul ever since I met you and received your good message. Only a man of your compassion and goodness can help me in this." She paused, her lower lip quivering. "I am not married to Bill Walsh. We are unwed, and living in sin before the eyes of God!"

Her words struck Smathers with the force of a hammer. He blinked in confusion and stepped hastily back from Candy. "Mrs. Walsh!" he whispered hoarsely. "What are you saying?"

"Call me Candy," she said, smiling suddenly. "I want you to call me that, Deacon Smathers. I do crave it so. From now on we must be honest with each other. So call me Candy, because I am not Mrs. Walsh. Will you?"

"Of course . . . Candy," he managed.

"Then you will help me to save myself from this awful sin?"

"Do you love this man you are living with?"

"I . . . thought I did, but now I'm unsure. Since meeting you, I have learned a deeper love. And now I fear I am lost . . . unless you can show me the way, Deacon—the way to God's love and forgiveness."

Smathers could hardly contain his joy. He felt an overwhelming rush of goodness toward this poor woman who wanted only God's forgiveness for her weakness. And he would be the agent of that forgiveness. He would lead her to the path of righteousness!

Boldly, he took both her hands in his. "Trust me . . . Candy. I will lead you from this unholy alliance. A new land awaits you, and with it a new life! I promise you!"

With an impulsive squeal of delight, Candy flung her arms around his neck and planted a kiss on the deacon's cheek. Then she turned and vanished into the darkness from which she had come. Smathers stood transfixed, the spot on his cheek where she had just kissed him glowing like a benediction.

Her hand up to her mouth to stifle her giggling, Candy peered cautiously out from behind a corner of her wagon as the deacon, obviously in a daze, turned and moved off toward the next campfire. Beside her, Bill Walsh was also holding back his laughter. The moment Smathers disappeared, Candy clambered swiftly into their wagon, Bill right behind her, then turned and collapsed in his arms. At once the two were convulsed with fits of laughter, and the wagon shook with their barely suppressed hilarity.

At last their mirth subsided, and they began to slap and punch each other in an intoxicating overabundance of high spirits. A dull, miserable trek was being transformed into one more game for them. They both were accomplished con artists, used to plying their trade among the gullible on the Mississippi River steamboats. But with the riverboats now mostly destroyed or sunk as a result of the war, they had moved on to Denver. But a con game had turned sour there, and they had made a hasty exit and now were on their way to the booming outpost of Seattle, hoping for greener plucking. Though they had joined up with the emigrant wagon train, they never had any intention of staying with it to the deacon's promised land—the Willamette Valley.

"I'm tellin' you, Candy," Bill said, wiping his eyes, "you'll have that gent talkin' to himself. He's a goner. What're you gonna do for an encore?"

Candy looked with sudden, mischievous intensity at her partner. "I'll make a bet with you, Bill Walsh."

Bill sobered instantly. He knew Candy was up to something, especially when she got that look in her eye. Trouble was, more often than not, the look meant trouble. "What're you up to, Candy?"

"A bet, that's what I'm up to. You willing?"

"Depends on the bet, sure enough." Eyes narrowing, he leaned close. "What you got cookin' in that head of yours, Candy?"

"I'm going to seduce Deacon Smathers."

"My God! You're crazy! He's a man of the gospel, and I never saw a one that took his role more serious. He'd fry in hell first."

"You ain't got that right, Bill."

"What do you mean?"

"He'll fry if he *don't*! I just set that poor bastard on fire."

"My, you *are* sure of yourself."

"He's a man, ain't he? Like you always said, there ain't a one that can't be made."

"Not this feller, Candy. Hell, you got him all set to save your soul, ain't you? How's he gonna save your soul if he's busy plowin' you?"

"That's just it, Bill. He ain't gonna save my soul. And just maybe he'll lose his own by trying."

Bill frowned suddenly. The whiff of damnation momentarily hovered over them both—it always did whenever Candy got into one of these moods. But he shook off the feeling as he marveled once again at his partner's audacity.

"All right," he told her. "It's a wager. So what are we betting?"

"If I bed that pious fool, you marry me and we settle down in Seattle, as man and wife."

"Hey now, Candy!"

"If I lose, I'll never devil you about it again."

"That a promise?"

Candy nodded emphatically.

"Then it's a bet."

With a delighted squeal, Candy grabbed Bill and kissed him full on his mouth, lingering awhile and exploring it with her tongue. When she pulled back, Bill did not want to let her go. And so he didn't.

Chapter 5

The rain that had teased them the day before became a full-fledged downpour during the night, and the wagon train resumed its trek toward the Grande Ronde River through a steady, dispiriting rain that turned breakfast into a wet misery and promised a noon stop equally gloomy.

The noon meal was exactly that, and the settlers were forced to pull up and remain within the dripping interiors of their wagons, gnawing on tough bread and salt pork. Settlers who had become accustomed to greeting each other heartily at every stop kept to themselves and remained hidden away in a vain attempt to escape the ceaseless, driving rain. Gradually, as they resumed their trek through the mountain valley, the wagons separated in the rain. And as the deep ruts in the wet ground pulled stubbornly on their wheels and the horses found their fetlocks suddenly heavy with clinging globs of mud, the wagons fell still farther apart.

The pelting rain persisted through the next day. But on the fourth day out of Baker the downpour slackened some, and close to sundown the deacon directed his lead wagon through a stand of hemlock and out onto the high bank that bordered the Grande Ronde River. Waiting for him was Matt Cord, who urged that they cross the river and put it behind them before camping for the night. But the wagons were strung too far apart, and by the time the stagecoach arrived, it was dark and too late to attempt a crossing.

They had no choice but to camp where they were. As the settlers climbed down from their wagons, the rain ceased entirely, and the sound of laughter once again could be heard as it rang across the meadow. Some even attempted campfires. Scott Winslow, however, was careful to keep to himself, not yet ready to confront his father's killer. The settlers had come almost fifty miles in three days and were pleased to have finally reached the banks of the Grande Ronde, especially when they considered the wet hell through which they had been forced to journey. Soon they all were bedded down peacefully for the night, lulled by the river's pleasant music.

They awoke to its roar.

Winslow didn't bother to shave, but dressed swiftly and gulped down a stale breakfast roll. Then, with the roar of the turbulent river ominously growing, he joined the rest of the settlers on the riverbank. They were crowded around Matt Cord and a very agitated Deacon Smathers.

An argument was in progress, with Matt Cord insisting that they must drive their wagons across the river immediately, before it rose any higher. Winslow wasted no time in leaving the group. The sight of Matt Cord unnerved him. A confusion of motives clashed within his breast, and he knew he had better put some distance between himself and this man he had hunted for almost four years.

Scott sought a knoll farther along the bank and studied the river. It had gained at least a foot overnight and was dark with silt as it furiously rushed past the promontory on which he stood. Branches and other debris were caught in its grasp, creating fearsome battering rams threatening anyone or anything that might attempt to negotiate the river at this time.

But Cord was right about one thing: The river would get much higher before it got any lower. Furthermore, there was every likelihood the rain would continue. Already a fine mist was falling. Recalling how wet the entire summer had been and how many swollen streams he had seen wherever he had ridden in this high country, Winslow realized that this last three-day cloudburst must have turned every mountain brook into what the Grande Ronde now was—a fierce and raging cataract.

Winslow heard someone approaching and turned to see Kate Harrow. She was wearing a long yellow slicker with a hood attached. Her face peering out at him from under the hood seemed flushed and surprisingly youthful. The warm glow of her complexion, he realized, was the combined result of her hurrying across the meadow to reach him and the moisture still heavy in the air. Nevertheless, Winslow was somewhat taken aback by the effect her appearance had on him.

She walked up beside him, then looked past him to the crowd around the wagon master and asked, "What's wrong?"

"The river is rising," he told her, looking back at the swollen waterway. "They're trying to decide whether or not to send the wagons across now, before it gets any higher."

Kate looked with renewed interest at the river and saw for the first time how it had risen during the night. She shuddered and looked back up at Winslow. "Do you think we can do that?"

"I doubt it. The river has risen at least half a foot since I've been standing here. But anything's possible."

"When will the river go down?"

Winslow glanced up at the sky. Dark clouds were rolling in once again, and the light mist was becoming heavier by the minute. "That's hard to say," he replied. "Not until this rain lets up, that's for sure. Then we'll have to wait for the river to hunker down some, and that'll take a while."

Kate frowned and shook her head. "That means we might have to stay here for some time."

"Yes, it does. Maybe a few days."

"And the girls are getting so restless."

Winslow heard the sound of sudden activity and looked back at the settlers crowding the riverbank. To his surprise, Smathers and a few of the settlers were busy unloading the preacher's crate of Bibles and other valuables, while in the wagon behind his, other settlers were helping Joshua Beechwood lighten his wagon as well.

At that moment, from Tim Curry's wagon, the tall woman, Samantha, rushed toward the riverbank. Tim caught up with her and led her quickly back from the water. From where Winslow stood, he could hear the woman's shrill cries. It sounded as if she was warning all of them. Glancing once more at the boiling river, Winslow wished those two fools still getting ready to cross would listen to the half-crazed woman. It might do them some good.

"Are they going to cross?" Kate asked, obviously surprised.

"That's what it looks like."

"But you said you didn't think we could make it now."

"I also said anything was possible."

As they stood watching the preparations, Matt Cord left the settlers and walked up the bank to where they were standing. Coming to a halt in front of Winslow, Cord smiled and stuck out his hand.

"I reckon you'd be the feller that made a mess of Bim Stagger's face back in Baker," he said grinning. It was not a pleasant grin.

Winslow forced himself to take the offered hand. "You'd be Matt Cord, then," he managed.

"That's right. The wagon master. We didn't get properly introduced last night."

"My name is Scott Winslow," Scott told him slowly, carefully, making sure Cord heard every syllable. "And this here is Kate Harrow."

Cord did his best not to smirk as he touched the brim of his hat and nodded at Kate.

Winslow had pronounced his name as slowly and distinctly as he had for a reason. But Winslow's name obviously had meant nothing to the wagon master—and at once Winslow was struck by the astonishing irony of his situation. He had just finished shaking the hand of the man who had killed his father. Yet all he felt was a dull, oppressive wonder that this scrawny, unkempt redhead with the receding chin should have been capable of slicing through Winslow's life with such devastating impact.

Cord turned his attention back to the preacher and Joshua Beechwood, who were climbing into their wagons. The river's ford was marked by a lightning-splintered pine on the near bank. With a high, almost comical yell, Smathers stood up and flicked his team's reins. Somewhat reluctantly, his two horses plunged into the swirling water, Beechwood's wagon following close behind.

It appeared at first that the river bottom was high and solid enough to enable the two wagons to make it across. But then a huge log appeared upstream, and it became obvious at once that it was going to strike either the deacon's or Beechwood's wagon broadside. A shrill warning erupted from the settlers on the bank. Smathers turned his head and saw the onrushing log. He slapped the reins onto the horses' backs and yelled furiously in an attempt to hurry them up, but the team caught only his panic and veered to the right. At once they were in water over their heads. Lunging frantically, they began swimming as they were swept even farther to the right. The wagon followed, left the ford, and began to drift downstream.

That was when the log slammed like a well-aimed battering ram into the side of the deacon's wagon. The sound of crunching wood came sharply to Winslow as he watched the wagon list heavily to the right and slump over, Smathers leaping into the water at the last minute. For a moment the deacon's head was visible as he was swept downstream. Then he disappeared below the boiling, swirling current.

"Let's go, Cord," Winslow cried, peeling off his shirt and hat as he raced toward the river. "That poor fool's gonna drown!"

Winslow sliced into the water well ahead of Cord, who didn't seem eager to risk his own neck. Winslow caught sight of the deacon as his dripping head emerged for a moment, and struck out for him at once. He caught up to Smathers just as a sudden whirlpool sucked the deacon under again. Winslow went down after him, grabbing frantically. As the man's churning leg struck Winslow a numbing blow on the side of the head, Winslow reached out and managed to get a firm grip on the deacon's shirt.

His lungs close to bursting, Winslow pulled for the surface, dragging the deacon up with him. As soon as they broke clear of the water, Winslow looked around for the shore. He caught sight of it—and of something else as well. Matt Cord was standing beside Kate Harrow on the shore, never even having entered the water. And it looked as if Kate was trying to get Scott's attention, frantically pointing downstream. Winslow turned in the direction she was indicating just in time to see an old cottonwood that leaned far out over the river, its gnarled trunk only inches from the surface of the water—and the surging flood was carrying Winslow toward it with express-train speed.

He ducked, but not soon enough. His head struck the tree a sickening blow. Losing his grip on the preacher, he felt himself being swept on down the river. So powerful had the blow on his head been that he was barely conscious, and though he was aware of a shrill, warning scream deep within his skull, he couldn't move his limbs. The dark, silty water enclosed him, pulling him into its sunless depths.

Suddenly, strong hands were pulling him from the river, then rolling him over onto his stomach. More hands—heavy, punishing—began beating on his back until he started coughing violently. A moment later, water dribbling out of his mouth, he opened his eyes to see Kate and Matt Cord bending anxiously over him.

Cord frowned down at him. "You all right, Winslow?"

Winslow managed a weak nod.

"Deacon Smathers is all right, too," Kate told him. "Thanks to you."

Winslow struggled to a sitting position. He was a mite dizzy and was aware that he had swallowed too much water. His chest felt heavy and his lungs burned. A strong hand caught him under his right arm and began to lift him to his feet. He glanced up to see who it was. Matt Cord.

The man smiled. "Looks like you owe me one, Winslow," he said. "You were going down for the third time, it looked like."

Winslow pulled himself free of Cord and struggled upright under his own power, a sudden unthinking fury consuming him. "Get away from me!" he snapped, his eyes blazing.

"Hey, what's the matter, Winslow?" Cord asked, stepping back hastily. "I'm only trying to help."

"I don't need your help. Touch me again and you'll wish you hadn't."

"Hell!" the man said, his face suddenly going mean. "Maybe I should have let you drown."

"Yes," Winslow said evenly. "Maybe you should have."

"Scott!" Kate cried, rushing to his side to calm him down. "What are you saying? This man saved your life!"

"Never mind, Miss Harrow," Cord said, his eyes narrowing thoughtfully. "I reckon he's still a little out of his head. He'll come around. I don't hold no grudge."

He smiled then at Winslow—a forced, troubled smile—and moved off with the still-groggy preacher. Winslow stepped back from Kate, the revulsion he had felt when Cord touched him still working on him. Only with difficulty could he manage a smile at Kate.

"Thanks, Kate. I guess I went off my head there. The preacher's all right, looks like. What about Beechwood?"

"He turned back in time. And they've retrieved the deacon's wagon and both his horses. It could have been much worse." She stepped a bit closer to Winslow and looked closely at him. "There's an awful welt on your forehead. Are you sure you're all right?"

"As soon as I get out of these wet clothes," he said, managing a grin.

"I'll walk back with you. You can change inside the stage." She smiled faintly. "I promise—I won't let any of the girls peek."

Winslow started across the meadow with her, absurdly—even resentfully—comforted by her presence. He was aware as he walked beside her that she had been deeply troubled by that violent outburst he had directed at

73

the wagon master. In her eyes it must have seemed completely uncalled for—and certainly unfair.

Winslow was unhappy about it as well, but for an entirely different reason. He had tipped his hand needlessly, since there was no doubt that from this point on the wagon master would be watching Winslow carefully and searching his mind for some clue as to why Winslow had reacted as he had. If the wagon master's slack mind had let the name of Ben Winslow fade into the dust of his murderous past, surely Scott's unprovoked outburst would set him to thinking just a mite harder about this man called Winslow— and why he should hate him so.

Perhaps, Winslow thought wearily, he should get his Colt and end this business right now. Why prolong it any longer? He had found the killer of his father. If to take him prisoner at this juncture was out of the question, then his only option was to call him out now and let his gun finish the job.

And yet it was no longer that simple, if it ever had been. For one thing, in a turn of fate so capricious it almost made Winslow laugh, Matt Cord had just saved his life. How did a man walk up to someone who had just done that and gun him down? Matt Cord might do such a thing, but could he?

Winslow shook his head wearily. It was strange how clear and direct everything had seemed when first he had imagined his final showdown with the highwayman who murdered his father. But no longer. His purpose and direction were now as muddy and as storm-swept as the water from which he had just been dragged.

74

Chapter 6

As the day wore on, the rain increased. After seeing what had happened to Deacon Smathers and what had almost happened to Joshua Beechwood, the settlers resigned themselves to remaining where they were until the rain let up, and they did their best to rainproof their wagons and make them habitable.

But the wagons were stuffed with trunks and favorite pieces of furniture, so much so that the only spaces left to the settlers for cooking and sleeping were considerably cramped. Because of the dampness and the lack of chimneys, there was precious little cooking attempted inside the wagons, and most of the settlers contented themselves with salt pork and bread with a few cans of cold beans, and perhaps some dried vegetables to add variety. The result was an increased irritability among the settlers.

The one who suffered most that second night by the river was Joshua Beechwood. That he easily could have precipitated a disaster by volunteering to cross the river with the deacon was something his wife, Amanda, was anxious he not forget. Over and over, with a tongue that grew sharper with use, she reiterated how outrageously stupid she considered him for having tried such a fool thing. What had he been thinking? she wanted to know. Was he really all that anxious to lose everything? What did he think would have happened to her if he and the wagon had been lost?

When Joshua was tardy in responding to that last question, Amanda lost no time in telling him: She would have become a burden to near strangers, a hostage to the wilderness. Had he no mercy for her? Was this her thanks for taking him back after what he had done? After the shame he had heaped upon her?

"Woman! Will you never cease your complaining?" Joshua demanded wearily, sitting up in their bed. As he did so, his head struck the corner of the ancient bureau she had insisted on taking with them.

"No!" Amanda spat. "Why should I? What have I got to be pleased about?"

Rubbing the sore spot on his head, Joshua sighed. "You could be pleased that I wasn't drowned and that our wagon is still intact. You could be pleased that we are on the way to a new country, to start our lives anew. It is what you told me you wanted."

"I wanted it because you told me it would help us forget the past—that it would help us begin again. At the time I convinced myself it was what I wanted as well. But I know better now. I was a fool, such a fool to take you back—to forgive you!"

With a weary sigh, Joshua said, "Why do you continue to say that, Amanda?"

"Because I believe it to be so."

"It seems to me you want it to be so."

"Yes," she snapped bitterly, glancing at him, her eyes aflame. "You are right, for once. It is because I want it to be so."

"No more of this, Amanda," Joshua pleaded, lying back down. "I warn you."

Amanda went silent, but he could feel her swelling with indignation beside him, all the venom she wanted to spit out bottling up inside her. She was fit to burst. She had wanted any excuse to let loose on him, and this morning's foolishness had given her that opportunity.

Yes, she *had* been a fool. And so had Joshua, he realized, to have thought she might one day forgive him his transgressions. Or to think that he would ever be able to explain to her why he had needed another woman's comfort. God knows he loved Amanda, and he was sure that in her own way she loved him too. But why couldn't she express that love more often in a physical way? Why did she make it so difficult for them to come together? Could she really be that indisposed, that sickly? And if so, was it his fault that he on the contrary was so healthy, with normal, healthy desires?

Joshua gritted his teeth and told himself to do something—to reach out to this woman beside him. After all, she was his wife. Perhaps he could soothe her and drain some of that bottled-up venom. His gentle hands had done this for many women. Why couldn't he do it for the woman he loved?

Bracing himself against the possibility of being repulsed, he reached out and placed his hand on Amanda's shoulder, desiring only to enclose her in his arms—to comfort her. But as he began to pull her toward him, she grew rigid. He increased the pressure slightly and called out softly to her. But she wrenched away from him and rolled over completely.

"Leave me be!" she cried. "I know what you want! That's all you think of! But I am not Annabel—I am not your whore!"

With a furious curse, Joshua flung his blanket back

and swiftly pulled his britches on. In a moment he was out of the wagon, leaning back against its side, the rain slanting down upon him. He welcomed its chill embrace—it matched his bitterness perfectly.

It was too wet for his pipe. Folding his arms, Joshua looked off in the direction of the stagecoach sitting among the pines. A ghostly cluster of tents surrounded the coach, and sleeping in those tents were women who understood the needs of a man. And damned if he was going to let *that* opportunity pass him by—not now, not after what that witch of his had just done to him. He was done with her. She didn't know it, but *he* did. And that was all that mattered.

Having made that decision, Joshua felt better—much better. He took a deep breath and lifted his face, letting the rain strike it full on, cooling the fire that scalded his soul.

Ah, Annabel! Annabel! he cried inwardly. *How I miss you tonight. You were right. I never should have gone back to her.*

Inside the wagon, Amanda dug her face into her pillow and began to weep uncontrollably. *What am I doing?* she cried to herself. *Why on earth am I driving Joshua away from me like this?* And when she was through weeping—when she finally felt as clean and as gutted as a discarded pea pod—with incredible, maddening perversity, she felt her hunger and deep need for her husband surging to life within her.

But he was gone—and besides, it was too late for that now.

Mary and Phil Turner were very young newlyweds. Mary—an auburn-haired girl with thick curls and hazel eyes and a babyish, uptilted nose—was seventeen. Her husband was nineteen. Their solidly built wagon was a present from Phil's father. Both sets of parents had stocked the wagon to the brim, and with their blessing the young-sters had set out with high excitement from a small town west of St. Louis to settle on the Pacific Coast.

That excitement was gone completely now.

Sitting up hugging his knees, Phil Turner watched Mary. Lying face down on their narrow bed, she was weep-ing again. He did not need to ask why. He knew she was lonesome for her brothers and sisters, for her friends back in Missouri. And most of all, she missed terribly her mother and father. Phil had long since given up trying to comfort her. As for himself, he was certain he had made the greatest mistake of his life. He wanted only to flee, to abandon Mary and this whole incredible undertaking. He saw no way that he could handle the responsibilities his marriage and this long, endless trek west had thrust upon him.

Early on, the Turners had lost their two head of cattle when both Jerseys, for no apparent reason, simply up and died on them. Soon thereafter, he found that he had com-pletely underestimated the feed his four enormous draft horses would need. If that weren't enough, the rear axle on their spanking new wagon had given way. Inexperienced in such matters, he had botched the axle's repair, with the result that they had been left behind by the wagon train they had first joined—a fine, populous train with plenty of wagons and a cavalry escort that virtually guaranteed their safety through Indian country.

It was because of his fumbling ineptness that the Turners found themselves part of this miserably small wagon train led by an emaciated, preoccupied deacon—and a wagon master Phil did not like or trust. It was now late in the season. There was little likelihood they would get through the mountains before snow fell. Now, like a pack of drowned rats, they were camped by a swollen, churning river that probably wouldn't subside for several weeks. And if that weren't enough, they were heading into the Blue Mountains without the cavalry escort that had promised to guard them against a renegade band of Indians rumored to be in the area.

Phil didn't see how he could hold on any longer. Already he had failed Mary by allowing that first wagon train to proceed without them. And he had failed in so many other ways as well. He was, he realized, a silly and bumbling fool, a snot-nosed kid masquerading as a grown-up. He didn't dare let himself dwell on the difficulties he would encounter building his own home and setting out alone to farm their homestead. How would they survive their first winter with nothing coming in? Purchasing what provisions they would need to tide them over was out of the question now, since he had been forced to spend on repairs and extra feed most of the capital his father had given him.

This growing, overwhelming sense of his own inadequacy had shaken him to the core. He saw no way that he could measure up—and he was absolutely certain that Mary's desire to return home was an indication that she, too, had sensed his appalling incompetence.

Now, watching his unhappy wife, he made no effort to comfort her. After all, how could he possibly give her the courage she needed to go on, when he himself was no longer a man, no longer even able to comfort her in bed as a man should? With a sigh, he reached down and pulled the blanket up over Mary, then grabbed his pillow and thrust it behind his back. Closing his eyes, he tried to sleep, allowing the steady patter of the rain upon the canvas to lull him.

Mary felt Phil pull the blanket up around her shoulders, and for just a moment thought he was going to slip back down in the bed beside her. Her entire body tensed with excitement—and hope. But in a moment she knew he wasn't going to rejoin her in the bed. She wiped her eyes and turned just enough to see him with his head leaning back against the side of the wagon, his eyes closed, apparently asleep.

It was her fault, of course, for carrying on as she had been doing. She had become such a weepy drudge. But Phil was such a little boy. Yes, that was what he was—a confused, moody, overgrown little boy. He bore no resemblance at all to the ebullient young man, so full of laughter and optimism, whom she had fallen in love with and married.

Now, cold and distant, a hesitant and fumbling lover, he uttered no more endearments. His kisses were dutiful, restrained, tentative. He completely had lost that earlier, passionate need for her. And now she was no longer certain that she loved him. But she needed him. Alone here in this wilderness with this boy the world called her husband, her only bulwark, her only protection—she felt defenseless and terribly vulnerable.

Oh, how foolish she had been to have married him!

And then she thought of his blond, curly hair, his laughably oversized ears that she had taken so much pleasure in teasing him about—and she began to weep again. She was so confused. One minute she felt only contempt for him, and the next she felt only a hopeless, painful love. With a bitter, sobbing sigh, she buried her head once more in her pillow and cried herself to sleep.

Ruth Whittington couldn't stop coughing. Noah sat up in the narrow bed and pulled her to a sitting position. Then, closing his arm around her, he hugged her gently.

"Lean back," he told his wife of forty-nine years. "Let these old bones warm you."

"Oh, Noah, am I keeping you awake?"

"I don't mind. It's you I'm worried about. I don't like the sound of that cough."

"In that case, I'll try to cough in a more pleasant manner."

He chuckled and squeezed her more tightly. She leaned her head into his shoulder and closed her eyes, his warmth filling her. She fought back a cough that threatened to break from her throat and sighed, grateful as always for Noah's strength. And for Noah.

Both the Whittingtons were aware of Mary and Phil Turner's problems adjusting to each other. The sad, heart-wringing sound of Mary's weeping could be heard even now from the next wagon. Ruth thought she knew what the trouble was and wished there were some way she could help. But she realized there was little anyone could do. Mary and Phil would have to work their way through this crisis on their own, just as she and Noah had done so many years before. It had not been easy for them either at the beginning. But the results, after all these years, had certainly been worth it.

And now here they were, realizing a lifelong dream. Their children were grown. Old friends had preceded them to the West Coast. And now at last they were going to join them and open a small general store in the Willamette Valley town of Salem. It would be such fun, Ruth told herself dreamily as the strong, bony arms of her husband clasped her to him. It would be just the two of them. Even if the store were to fail, it wouldn't bother her. Just being with Noah was enough. After so many years, each day the Lord gave them together was a blessing—a bonus she had never dreamed would be theirs.

She snuggled still closer to Noah.

"Are you comfortable, Ruth?" he asked gently.

"I'm fine," Ruth told him just as softly. "Thank you, Noah."

He answered her with a gentle squeeze. No longer coughing, Ruth fell into a deep, restful sleep.

On the fourth day of waiting beside the rain-swollen Grande Ronde River, Scott Winslow looked up from his poker hand in surprise. Outside the stage, someone wanted to see him, and he recognized the voice as that of Tim Curry, the young Johnny Reb. Tim was asking one of Kate's girls where he could find Mr. Scott Winslow.

Kate, sitting across from him, also looked up from her poker hand. Beside Kate, Dr. Throckmorton groaned slightly.

"No distractions, please," he murmured as he carefully fanned the cards he had just been dealt and proceeded to study them.

Winslow put his hand face down on the rough board serving as a table and leaned his head out the window—but not too far, for the rain was still pelting down. Curry, a rifle in his hand, was standing in front of Terry Lambert's tent, speaking with her. The instant Winslow saw Tim Curry's face, he realized the young man was hopelessly flustered. It was also evident that Terry knew precisely what effect she was having on him—and was pushing it to the hilt, all stops out.

"Mr. Winslow's playing cards with Kate and the doctor right now," Terry told the young man, smiling sweetly and moving still closer to him. "I'll tell you what. Why don't you wait inside my tent where it's nice and warm? They ought to finish the game soon—in a couple of days, anyway."

"Days? Oh, I . . ." And then Curry caught on. His blush was so flamingly vivid, it might have been used to turn a bull. Tim swallowed and looked helplessly away—and caught sight of Winslow peering out the stage window at him.

At once he started for the stage, but Terry caught his arm. In his surprise, Curry almost dropped his rifle. "What's the matter, Johnny Reb? Don't you want to come in out of the rain? You afraid of me?"

"Of course not," Tim replied in a fluster.

"Then it's something about *me* you don't approve of, is that it?"

"No, ma'am," Tim said, swallowing again, but his gaze now as steady as his voice. "I would like to go in that tent with you. I surely would. And thank you for invitin' me—it was right kind and thoughtful of you. I guess you could tell right off how much I . . . I . . . well, doggone it, I'll just say it: how much I like you. But that ain't no reason for you to make fun of me, Miss Terry. I can't help it if I'm taken by you. There ain't much a guy like me can do when a woman as pretty as you comes at me like you just did. But I'm sorry—right now I got other business to attend to."

Terry was momentarily taken aback. Tim's straightforward words had shamed her. Confused and perhaps even moved by Tim's sincerity, she found herself with no way to respond properly. So she slapped him. Hard.

"Terry!" Kate cried, opening the stage door and stepping out into the rain. "That was inexcusable! Apologize to Mr. Curry!"

Instead, tears streaming down her face, Terry turned and flung herself into her tent.

Winslow stepped quickly from the stage and restrained Kate. "Leave her be," he told her. "I think she's already been punished enough. Get on back inside the stage and out of the rain," Winslow prompted, "while I see what Tim wants."

Kate nodded and climbed back into the stage. Winslow took Tim's arm and directed him over to the protection of the pines.

"I see you got that new rifle with you," Winslow commented. "A Henry repeater. What've you got in mind?"

"I been seeing lots of deer sign, Mr. Winslow."

Winslow nodded. "I've been seein' lots of deer."

"And we're runnin' low on food," Tim continued quickly. "The whole wagon train is. Why don't you and me go do ourselves some huntin'?"

That wasn't a bad idea, Winslow realized. The very thought had occurred to him more than once as he saw the deer flitting through the gloomy, rain-soaked pines. The hunt would be a wet business, indeed, but anything was preferable to this interminable waiting—and to the constant debate within him concerning the fate of Matt Cord.

"I'll get my rifle," he told Curry, "and be with you in a minute."

Before he left, Winslow poked his head into the stage. "I'm folding. Tim and I are going hunting. You want to join us, Doctor?"

"My dear sir," Throckmorton replied. "What a glorious prospect, especially in this lovely weather. But as you know, my gout is beginning to act up again—fearfully and suddenly. I must ask you to forgo the pleasure of my company on such a merry, and I hope profitable, expedition. Another time, perhaps?"

Winslow grinned. "I'll be looking forward to that, Doctor." With a quick wave to Kate, he left them.

Of course, now that they were on the hunt, all game had miraculously vanished from the woods. For at least two hours they moved through the drenching woodland, and when at last they pulled up on the edge of a clearing, Winslow found himself thinking longingly of that warm, dry, comfortable seat he had abandoned in the stagecoach.

"Maybe it's because of these slickers," Tim said. "They're too bright."

"You want to go on without them?" Winslow asked, taking off his hat and swinging it wide to get rid of the water trapped in the brim.

"Nope," said Tim wearily. "Let's keep goin'."

"Maybe we'd do better keeping still," Winslow suggested, gazing out over the placid meadow. The lush grass was almost blue in the wet light. "We can't do any worse than we've been doing, and it's a hell of a lot easier."

Tim nodded. "Sounds like a good idea," he admitted.

A towhead of twenty-five, Tim Curry looked considerably younger, with wide blue eyes and a clean-shaven, youthful face. Though he had been moving through the woodland without too much apparent difficulty, a wound he had sustained at Shiloh had permanently crippled his left leg, leaving it half its original heft and apparently quite weak. But Tim was unwilling to make excuses and had kept up with Winslow's long, easy strides without a murmur.

A habit he had of taking out his harmonica and playing it at the close of day—often while the campfires died and the train's occupants readied themselves for sleep—had endeared him to every member of the wagon train, especially to Kate's girls. On one occasion that Winslow remembered, however, the effect on one listener had not been so benign. Melody Tinsdale, after hearing Tim play "When Johnny Comes Marching Home," flung herself into her tent, weeping bitterly. When Kate gave up trying to calm the girl, there were tears in her own eyes as well. It seemed that Melody mourned her own, real soldier named Johnny, who would never come marching home.

Now, as the two men stood in the deep grass at the edge of the rain-soaked meadow, Tim revealed to Winslow why he was on this trek to Oregon—alone except for the crazed elderly woman he had met in Fort Boise.

After being released from the army hospital, Tim had

deserted the Confederate cause and set out with his mother to reach the Willamette Valley, where her brother was already homesteading. The trek was uncommonly difficult, however, with miserable weather. A few weeks before they reached Fort Boise, his mother died of scarlet fever. Tim buried his mother on the trail, and when he reached the fort he saw a woman who vaguely resembled her, rocking ceaselessly in front of the troopers' barracks. Twice she had waved to him as he passed her. Curious, Tim had inquired about her and her odd behavior.

Her story, as he learned later, was not an unusual one for these parts, but it had appalled and riveted him nevertheless.

A tall, gaunt woman, Samantha Ridley was forty when she and her husband and six-year-old girl were attacked by a war party of four Blackfoot braves while on their way through the Idaho wilderness to Oregon. Without warning, the Indians' arrows toppled her husband from the wagon seat, and before she could grab the reins, the fierce unearthly yells of the war party stampeded the horses until the wagon broke up on the rough ground, flinging her and her daughter free.

At once they were captured and taken back to watch while the Blackfoot warriors began to kill her husband— slowly—using arrows to stab him repeatedly. When the little girl broke free of her mother and ran in horror from the sound of her father's screams, a young brave caught up with her and crushed her blond head with one blow of his war hatchet. The crumpled body was flung at the woman's feet, while the savage who had performed this atrocity danced around her, shouting out devilish chants.

Something snapped inside the woman. The sight of her husband bound by rope to a tree, dozens of arrows hanging limply from his bloody, naked body, was more than she could bear. And the death of her little girl aroused her to a fury that drove from her all thought of caution and all fear.

Screaming in fury, she rushed upon the brave dancing around her. Snatching his long hunting knife from its deerskin sheath, she plunged it hilt-deep into his chest. Withdrawing the knife, she flung herself at the nearest Indian, slashing his throat so severely that his head fell back loosely, hanging by a single bloody flap. Bathed now in the streaming blood of this decapitated brave, she snatched up the hatchet he had been carrying, fell upon the next Indian, and with one stroke split his skull, opening it like a ripe melon. The remaining brave halted his torment of her dying husband, grabbed his pony, and galloped off into the wilderness. The Blackfoot had seen enough to realize that this woman was now more than a mere mortal. Madness had joined her spirit with that of the Great Spirit. With such medicine, she was now clearly invincible—and holy.

To the Gosiute, also, she was holy. She wandered into their camp a few weeks later, babbling and crying, her clothing in tatters, the dried blood of her victims still staining her arms and nearly naked torso. A few Gosiute braves backtracked along the woman's trail and from the signs left behind, were able to read this woman's fearsome tragedy as if from the pages of a book. They buried what was left of her husband and little girl, then returned to their camp, where they kept Samantha Ridley in a special lodge until they felt she was strong enough to be brought to Fort Boise. Meanwhile, the mountain men who hunted and trapped in the surrounding mountains heard her story and spread it among the Shoshone and other tribes that inhabited the region, so that by the time Samantha finally reached Fort Boise, she was a legend.

As Tim finished Samantha's story, Winslow nodded. "Yes, I heard of her," he remarked softly. "And I heard of another woman, some years ago. As I understand it, this other woman refused to leave the burial site of her husband and children and was kept alive by donations from Crow Indians, who regarded her as a holy woman.'' Winslow shook his head and sighed. "I suppose it will happen again. A person just can't stand to see loved ones done to death in that fashion. It breaks them. And the Indians know that, I'm sure."

"Samantha's better now," Tim said. "Much better. When I began talking to her at the fort, she smiled and almost seemed to know me from somewhere." He smiled, almost shyly. "Do you think she could have read the sorrow in my face—that somehow she knew about my mother's death?"

"Stranger things have happened, Tim," Winslow said. "I've heard it said that sorrow is the universal language."

"Yes," Tim said thoughtfully. "I suppose so. Well, I was lonely, and I could see she was. I still had all my mother's things, so I asked her if she wanted to continue her journey west with me, and she nodded. But I could see on the day we left that she didn't want to leave her rocker behind, so I made room in the wagon for that as well. Now, whenever we stop and the weather is good enough, I take it down for her and let her rock. She seems to like that."

"Yes, she does," agreed Winslow. "We've all seen her—and the rest of us like that harmonica of yours, as well."

Tim smiled. "I guess you don't have any choice." He shivered and shook his head to get rid of the moisture piling up on his hat brim, then looked quickly around. "But right now we've got a choice—whether to drown or freeze to death. If we don't get lucky soon, I think maybe we'd better turn around and get back to the wagons."

"Patience," Winslow counseled softly. "Patience. We've been standing here less than half an hour."

Gloomily, Tim nodded and shifted his weight to his good leg.

"Don't move," said Winslow, his voice barely audible. "And don't speak."

But Winslow hadn't needed to say a thing to Curry as the buck—a ten pointer at least—seemed to appear like an apparition out of the shifting curtains of rain obscuring the far side of the meadow. It was a black-tailed deer, larger than a mule deer, with glowing, yellowish red on its breast and belly.

Both men, as silent and as immobile as statues, watched the buck's stately approach, its antlered head moving quickly from side to side in its search for possible predators. Still well out of rifle range, the buck halted and looked back at the edge of the clearing from which it had emerged. At once a doe and a yearling stepped out of the timber after it, moved swiftly into the meadow, and proceeded to browse.

Then it was the buck's turn to browse. The moment its head ducked, both men raised their rifles and stepped closer. They moved stealthily forward until a whisk of the buck's black tail alerted them. They froze as the deer's head shot up alertly. It looked directly at them for a long moment, gazed to their right, then swept the clearing. It had seen them, but since they hadn't moved, the deer regarded them as nothing more dangerous than a tree or a queer stand of brush.

The buck resumed its browsing. Winslow and Tim edged closer to the feeding animal, being careful to move in such a way that any instant halt on their part would pose no difficulty. Twice more the deer was alerted, and each time it gazed carefully at the two frozen riflemen for a moment or so, then looked swiftly about, dropped its head, and resumed its feeding.

Within range at last, Winslow aimed carefully and fired. To his dismay, he only managed to powder one of the antlers. But beside him, Tim Curry fired at the already moving animal and brought it down. Then, to Winslow's amazement, Tim levered swiftly and flung a second shot at the rear of the plunging doe, bringing it down as well.

Winslow glanced with new appreciation at his hunting companion. "That's some rifle you got there, Tim. And you sure know how to use it."

"I've had plenty of practice, Scott," Tim replied. "But you're right—this Henry is a fine weapon. The Union has it now. Maybe that's another reason why the Confederacy is lost."

"I'd like to examine it more closely later, Tim."

"Anytime."

They hastened into the clearing to procure the fresh meat they had just harvested.

A good three hours later, as the two men stepped out of the pines beside the stagecoach with the doe slung around Tim's neck and the buck around Winslow's, a fortuitous rift in the clouds allowed a golden shaft of sunlight to bathe them and the rest of the encampment in its heartening glow.

It was an omen. Soon the rain would cease entirely, everyone agreed as they eagerly crowded around the successful hunters, and they would be across the river and on their way once again.

Tim nodded happily, as pleased as the rest, then hurried to put down his burden. He was anxious to find Terry Lambert and apologize to the girl. He hadn't meant to upset her like that.

Chapter 7

The rain stopped that night, and three days later the river was low enough for the wagon train and stagecoach to move across.

Earlier, on the occasion of that first foolhardy attempt to cross the river, Winslow had been astonished and even somewhat outraged at the careless, unplanned manner in which the deacon and Beechwood had been allowed to charge out into that raging flood. That Matt Cord had done nothing to dissuade them disturbed him almost as much as the attempt itself.

At the time it had not been easy for Winslow to keep his own counsel, and as events proved, he should have spoken out. This time he was determined that, if Matt Cord again failed in his job, he himself would see to it that the crossing was accomplished in a safe and prudent manner. As a stage driver for years under the tutelage of his father, Winslow knew that none in the wagon train need fear the loss of their wagon or their possessions if certain simple safeguards were followed. But watching the wagons lining up to cross, it soon became apparent that once again Matt Cord wasn't doing his job.

Right behind the deacon's lead wagon were Noah and Ruth Whittington, and Winslow watched as they calmly drove their team toward the river's edge, totally unaware of what lay ahead. It was as if they were on a Sunday afternoon outing, about to drive across nothing more troublesome than a deep puddle. Galvanized by this sight and no longer mindful of consequences, Winslow swiftly armed himself and hurried down to where the wagons were lining up. He planted himself directly in front of the deacon's wagon, his rifle resting casually in the crook of his right arm, his big Colt heavy on his hip.

"Hold up right there, preacher," Winslow said.

Riding on his horse alongside the deacon's wagon was Matt Cord, seemingly as innocent of danger as any of the others.

"What the hell you up to, Winslow?" the wagon master demanded.

"I think you'd better tell this wagon train to hold up. This isn't the proper way to cross a river—not when it's still this high."

"Stand aside, Winslow. I'm the wagon master here."

"Nevertheless, I'm telling you to hold up."

Leaning forward over his pommel, Cord let his hand drop to the butt of his six-gun. He smiled coldly. "You want I should make you get out of our way, Winslow?"

"Go for your weapon, Cord," Winslow said quietly, "and I'll blast you out of that saddle. It'll be just the excuse I've been looking for."

Cord's chinless face paled as he quickly leaned back in his saddle, careful to keep both hands in view.

Winslow looked back at the astonished Deacon Smathers. "You better not cross this soon unless you take

93

a few precautions, preacher. And I aim to see that you take those precautions.''

''Matt's right, Winslow,'' the deacon said. ''You're out of line. Matt's already told me that we can cross now—as long as we stay on the ford. He plans to ride ahead and lead the way.''

Winslow took a deep breath. Telling such a fool as this cleric not to be one was as useless as whistling in a gale. So he wouldn't try.

''All right then, preacher,'' Winslow told him, smiling thinly. ''Let Cord show you the way. Might be a good idea at that—for you and Cord, that is. But I'm not going to let the rest of the wagons follow you.''

Smathers considered that option for a moment. Then, with a nervous glance past Winslow at the still-swift water, he snapped, ''All right, then. Just what precautions would you have us take?''

Winslow smiled. ''Glad to see you take that attitude. I suggest you get down here and gather the rest of your flock. I don't want to have to repeat myself, and I'll be needing some volunteers.''

A moment later, Winslow led the deacon and the rest of the settlers to a shady spot on the riverbank. Hunkering down at the foot of a tree, he began his dissertation, occasionally drawing on the ground with a stick to illustrate the points he was making. It didn't escape Winslow's notice that throughout his long recital Matt Cord paid no attention whatsoever to what he was saying. Instead, the wagon master studied Winslow with his dead, soulless eyes. And at last a slow light of understanding lit the man's ferretlike face.

Winslow's common-sense advice was followed, and soon preparations to cross began. As he pointed out to the settlers, after a period of flooding, the fording places of a river often shift or become clogged with loose sand deposited by the action of the undercurrent. As a result, it was imperative that someone first go across on foot to ascertain the exact location and condition of the ford.

Joshua Beechwood volunteered for this task. As he started across the Grande Ronde, the water in places almost up to his waist, he planted sticks wherever the sand was sufficiently solid, until he had marked the ford's location. To the surprise of everyone but Winslow, the ford had indeed shifted. It now slanted sharply downstream. But this was a happy circumstance, as Winslow was quick to point out, since now it wouldn't be necessary for the wagons to buck head on the still-rapid flow of the river.

After the ford had been traced, Winslow sent Phil Turner and Bill Walsh to shore up the opposite bank with brush and fresh earth. Once that task was completed, the horses were watered thoroughly to make sure they wouldn't stop to drink upon entering the stream. For if they should pause, the wagons would swiftly become bogged down.

The first wagon—the deacon's—was driven across by Scott Winslow, with Smathers crouching behind him in the wagon. Tim Curry walked in front of the team, guiding them with a rope. Joshua Beechwood rode on horseback on the downstream side of the wagon, his whip ready to keep the horses moving at as brisk a pace as possible. In like fashion, each wagon was driven across by Winslow and safely parked along the far shore. Then it was time for Kate's stagecoach. There was a bit of excitement when, halfway across, it looked as if the stage's narrow wheels were about to get dangerously mired in the treacherous sand. But Winslow's snapping bullwhip got the final ounce of pull from his four steeds, and the stagecoach, wallowing unsteadily, climbed the far bank and came to rest, its bright woodwork now a sad, muddy smear.

The crossing completed, a startling discovery was made: The wagon master had disappeared.

It was an excited Deacon Smathers who brought the news to Winslow, who had been in the act of climbing up into the stagecoach's box. Climbing back down, he turned to face the deacon, a frown on his face. "You sure of this?" he asked.

"Noah Whittington saw him leaving, and when the old man tried to stop him, Matt knocked him down and rode off, laughing."

Winslow frowned in sudden concern. "Noah? Why was Noah trying to stop Matt?"

"Because Matt was riding off on Noah's best horse—said his own mount had pulled up lame during the crossing. As far as Noah is concerned, Matt's no better than a horse thief. Noah has sworn to keep his rifle primed and ready in case Matt ever shows up again."

Winslow smiled grimly at old Noah's crust, while he tried to digest this unsettling news. He tried to understand what it was he felt. Anger, frustration—or was it relief? He couldn't be sure.

"I guess I don't blame Noah," Winslow said. "But what about you, Deacon? You about ready to write off that excuse for a wagon master?"

The deacon didn't hesitate. "I am."

"And you plan to go on without him?"

"What choice do we have? We have come this far, and going back across that river isn't a pleasant prospect."

"There are Indians in these mountains, Deacon. And not very pleasant ones at that. It might be dangerous to go on."

"It has been a dangerous journey from the start, Mr. Winslow. We have heard rumors of hostile Indians almost from the beginning, but that hasn't stopped us. We will not give up. God will protect us. We are his children. We have come this far, and we will go on."

Winslow nodded. "All right, then. But we'd better

get started. We want to get through Deadman's Pass before the rains turn to snow.''

Winslow turned back to the stage and climbed up into his box. Deacon Smathers, still standing below him on the ground, cleared his throat. Winslow glanced down at the man. "What is it now, Deacon?"

"Mr. Winslow," the deacon began, somewhat nervously. "I was hoping you would consent to becoming our new wagon master."

"You sure you know what you're saying?"

"I've already spoken to the others, and the vote was unanimous, Mr. Winslow. We would appreciate very much if you would consider yourself the new wagon master."

"What if Matt Cord comes back?"

"I doubt he will. But if he does, he'll first have Noah Whittington to answer to—and we know what *he'll* do to him." There was a slight smile on the deacon's face.

Winslow laughed and picked up the ribbons. "All right," he told the cleric. "I'm your new wagon master. But it's on one condition."

"Name it."

"This here stagecoach—containing Kate Harrow and her daughters of Venus—will lead the wagon train."

The preacher blanched, then nodded briskly. "As you say, Mr. Winslow. Proceed at once to the head of the wagon train. I shall tell the others to wait for Miss Harrow's stage to get in position."

Matt Cord drove the horse he had stolen from Noah Whittington without rest and without mercy. It had become a stumbling, heaving brute, its flanks ribboned with dried lather, by the time Cord finally reached Red Feather's encampment late the same day.

He was stopped at the same place he had been on his first visit, but this time the mounted braves who greeted him were even less friendly. The insolent brave who first had called him Crooked Face galloped straight up to Cord and swung up his bronzed arm. It struck Cord with the unforgiving impact of a tree branch, knocking him off his horse. Landing hard, Cord scrambled to his feet, his right hand reaching for his Colt. Before he could draw the weapon, however, the brave flung himself off his horse and swung a second time, again knocking Cord to the ground.

Desperate, confused, and more than a little outraged at this uncalled-for assault, Cord bleated, "What the hell's wrong with you? Take me to see Red Feather! You can't treat me like this!"

The Indian stepped back while four other braves, still mounted, closed in around them. "Yes I can, Crooked Face. When I show Red Feather how you treat your horse, he will slap you too, I bet." Then he turned, swung up onto his pony, and looked back at Cord. "We lead your horse into camp. You walk. But you best not keep Red Feather waiting. Already he wait too long for wagon train."

Senses reeling, a feeling close to panic building within him, Cord stumbled after the five Indians. He had left the wagon train because he finally had realized who Scott Winslow was—and the knowledge had congealed his blood. He had considered bushwhacking Winslow, but knew he wasn't up to it. Something about Winslow warned him that he wouldn't be easy to take.

So as soon as he could manage it, he had lit out for the camp of his ally, Red Feather—and this was the reception he got!

Red Feather was standing in front of his lodge, waiting for Cord. His face revealed as much emotion as a weathered cliff when the weary Cord came to a halt in front of him.

"I came to tell Red Feather what happened to the

wagon train,'' Cord huffed. ''But I've just been beaten by one of your braves! I demand you punish him!''

''First Cord will tell Red Feather where the wagon train has gone. We are not far from the pass, but there is no wagon train. We wait for too long already, I think. Have you made deal with horse soldiers, Cord? Are you a white man, after all?''

''Dammit! The rain stopped us at the Grande Ronde. There was nothing I could do. I tried to get them across before the river got too high, but it went bad.''

''You could have ridden across alone and warned us of delay. Many of my braves leave already. They say you trick Red Feather.''

Cord looked narrowly at Red Feather. Something was wrong, he suddenly realized—very wrong. Whenever this wily, well-educated half-breed spoke in a chopped, sarcastic dialect, it meant trouble. It meant he was toying with Cord, who looked nervously around. He tried to swallow, but his mouth had gone so dry that he couldn't get the spittle past his gullet.

''Why, hell, Red Feather,'' he managed, ''you must have enough braves to get the job done. There ain't that many in the train, and they should reach the pass in two more days at the latest. That should give you plenty of time to get those braves of yours back. Then they will see that Matt Cord did not trick Red Feather.''

By the time Cord finished his speech, he was perspiring profusely. Beads of sweat were coursing down his forehead and his armpits were sopping wet. But Red Feather didn't reply. His face remained impassive, his cold eyes inscrutable.

Cord became aware then that Red Feather's entire force had ridden up silently behind him. He could hear the horses blowing and the occasional whisk of their tails. The squaws, too, had come out to watch and stood in a line off to his right. Some were smiling almost shyly at him. Others were looking at him the way a vulture might a snared rabbit.

Taking a deep breath, Cord looked Red Feather squarely in the face. "You do what I just said, Red Feather," he managed, "and you won't regret it. You can trust me. That wagon train'll be there in a couple of days."

"Good," Red Feather said. He almost smiled, then nodded slightly at a brave sitting on his horse behind Cord.

A rawhide lariat fell around Cord's shoulders. Before he could slip out of its grasp, it tightened brutally around his biceps and he was yanked sharply to the ground. He landed on the small of his back and gasped out in sudden pain. Twisting around, he saw at the other end of the lariat the same Indian who had tormented him earlier.

"Hey, now, Red Feather," Cord pleaded. "There ain't no call for you to go and do this. I told you. I been levelin' with you. Let me up now!"

"Tall Fox will take you to his squaw," Red Feather told him. "He does not like you. It will give him pleasure to see you serve his squaw and her mother. Grant is no longer in our camp. He went completely mad and escaped, I am afraid. Now you will be the one to show us how a white man can crawl and howl in pain."

Cord tried desperately to free himself from the lariat, but before he could, Tall Fox swung his pony around and at a full gallop dragged Cord across the ground toward his lodge. By the time they arrived at the campfire Tall Fox's squaw was tending, Cord was nearly unconscious. A thorn bush and a boulder had treated him cruelly, the latter almost crushing his skull.

But Tall Fox's squaw soon brought him around. She pulled the lariat off Cord's shoulders and applied a burning brand to his crotch. As Cord leaped up, clutching at his groin in horror, Tall Fox's ancient mother knocked him back to the ground with a heavy war club her son had given her. The rest of the squaws crowded around and shrieked out their delight—and then eagerly plunged their own brands into the campfire.

Watching the squaws, Red Feather smiled, then turned to Tall Fox as the brave dismounted before him.

"We move out tomorrow and wait in the pines above the pass," Red Feather told him. "The wagon train will reach it in two days. Crooked Face was too terrified to have lied."

Then Tall Fox turned to the eighteen mounted braves that still remained in the camp and spoke to them in their own tongue, telling them what they had been waiting to hear. When he had finished, they raised their rifles and shouted to the sky.

But their yelling barely drowned out the terrified, yelping screams that came almost continuously now from Matt Cord's writhing figure.

Winslow studied an itinerary the army had provided Deacon Smathers. It read: *Cedars on bluffs. Grass and wood all the way up the trail from river. Water in parkland rimmed with cottonwood. Good camp.* The next entry read: *Seven miles. Trail over ridge to meadow. Then parkland. Water and good grass. Deadman's Pass west end of parkland.*

Winslow handed the itinerary back to the deacon, who took it and folded it carefully before returning it to his pocket. "We're right on schedule, looks like," he told Smathers. "Just over seven miles to the pass. We should reach it easily by tomorrow afternoon. I suggest we keep on going through it and camp on the other side."

"I agree," the deacon replied. "We'll feel much better with the pass behind us—and the Willamette Valley ahead."

"Yes," Winslow agreed, smiling. "I imagine we will, at that."

The deacon left then, and Winslow watched him for a while before continuing on through the cedars to the river. They had made camp less than an hour before, and already the cedars were fragrant with woodsmoke and the savory smell of fresh meat roasting on spits. Coming out of the cedars, he found himself close by Tim Curry's wagon.

In her rocking chair in front of it sat Samantha Ridley. As he passed her, she nodded to him—and kept right on rocking. Winslow couldn't be sure, but he thought she was humming the hymn "Nearer My God to Thee."

That was indeed the hymn Samantha Ridley was singing to herself.

Now that the rain had stopped and they were lifting into the high, clear air of the mountains, a strange and frightening clarity had fallen over her. The land around her seemed achingly familiar. Faces and sounds long dormant stirred to life within her—vague tentative shards that scratched at the back of her mind, threatening to break through like the beaks of tiny chicks pecking out through their shells. But there was something fearsome about these chicks—something dark and horrible. She dared not close her eyes, lest she see them more clearly.

The thought caused her heart suddenly to beat faster. To still its frenzied beating, she hummed just a little louder. Terrible things had been prowling just beyond the threshold of her consciousness for so long that she couldn't remember a time when she hadn't been on guard against them.

It was the rocking that had saved her. It shook the memories back into her past. They couldn't break through as long as she kept on rocking. Still, despite the beauty of this sunny afternoon in late autumn, the ugly and horrifying memories were pecking out through her fragile shell once more. Evil memories. Painful. Bloody.

Samantha shuddered and began to rock even faster, her humming gaining a notch in volume. But the hymn and the rocking couldn't still the birds in the cedars behind her or the wind in the pines or the feel of the golden sunlight on her face. Life was bursting in upon her with all its wonder— and all its terrible pain.

Tears began to course down her cheeks. She heard dimly her little girl's terrified scream. And she began to rock still faster. And faster.

Chapter 8

Deadman's Pass beckoned in the distance, a welcome break in the series of snowcapped peaks that shouldered into the bright afternoon sky. A long, narrow ridge on the western flank of the pass was covered with a thick stand of pine and reminded Winslow of a Mohawk Indian's scalp lock. The sheer walls of the pass almost seemed to have been sliced out of the mountain by the strokes of a monstrous ax.

"A mighty pretty sight, that," Throckmorton pronounced. "Yes, indeed. I wonder the poets have not captured this in appropriate verse."

"Perhaps you should try it, Doctor," Winslow commented wryly, the ribbons trembling in his hands.

"Indeed! You flatter me, sir."

Laughing gently, Winslow glanced back. The evenly spaced wagons filled the gently sloping parkland with dust as they rolled toward the distant pass, like a fleet of schooners approaching a mist-shrouded channel. As his eyes swept off to the right, he saw a herd of antelope moving off in long, soaring leaps. It truly was beautiful country.

When he turned back around, the doctor asked, "How long will it take us to reach the pass, do you think?"

Winslow considered a moment. "An hour, I should say."

"Capital! Then we should be through it long before we make camp. We will have beaten the snows."

"We're not through it yet, and there'll be some hard going before we start down the other side."

"Spoilsport," the doctor growled, reaching into his black bag for his medicinal spirits.

With less than a mile to go before the stage entered the pass, Winslow thought he saw a bear in the tall grass a quarter mile ahead. The animal appeared to be making directly for the stagecoach and was doing its best to maintain an upright position. Winslow found himself recalling the Indian name for the bear: The Animal That Walks Like A Man.

Reaching for his Sharps, Winslow checked the load and then let the weapon rest across his knees, all the while playing the ribbons as expertly as before. With a curious sidelong glance, the doctor stirred to life. He had been dozing.

"What in tarnation are you readying that cannon for, Winslow?" he demanded.

Instead of replying, Winslow pointed toward the bear still bounding through the grass toward the stage. Even as he pointed out the animal, it changed its direction slightly, as if deciding to come upon them from the front. A true rogue bear, Winslow reflected. It seemed bent on bringing down one of the stage's horses, perhaps. He had heard of grizzlies attacking horses. His father had told him of losing a powerful Belgian gelding to a renegade grizzly early one spring on a run through the Rockies.

But hell, this bear was no grizzly!

Alarmed, Winslow pulled up, yanking with sudden haste on the reins. Behind him, he heard the sound of wagons pulling up also. Caught off guard, many of the drivers were forced to shout out commands to their team as they sawed frantically on their reins.

From below, Kate called out, "What is it, Scott? Why are we stopping?"

"Nothing to fear, Kate," Throckmorton calmly replied. "We are just stopping to pick up a grizzly. He must have missed an earlier stage."

"What?" shrieked Kate.

By this time Winslow was on his feet, his palm shading his eyes as he peered into the bright grassland ahead of them. And this time he knew for damn sure it was no grizzly.

"Stay here," he told Throckmorton needlessly, as he swiftly clambered down off the stage and started to run through the grass.

From behind him, he heard a horse galloping and turned to see Tim Curry atop his gray.

"What is it, Scott?" Tim called as he pulled up alongside Winslow.

"Can't you see him? Over there—to your right. Coming at us through the grass."

Tim swung his gaze to the right, searched for a moment, then gasped. "I see it!" he cried. "Some kind of an animal. A bear, more than likely."

"Bear, hell! Since when does a bear have a beard? It's some poor sonofabitch out there racing to meet us! And what he's doing out here, I'd like to know. Come on!"

Winslow ran steadily, Tim holding his mount to a canter beside him. Abruptly, from out of the tall grass, the apparition burst upon them, more startling in appearance close up than he had been from a distance. His arms and legs were black with filth, and his ravaged, bearded face was as dark as an Indian's. What clothing remained on his skeletal torso and legs was at best in tatters, and there were no shoes on his bloodied feet.

Striding swiftly forward, Winslow caught the fellow in his arms a moment before he collapsed.

"Name's Grant," the man gasped. "Thomas Grant. Must . . . warn you! Red Feather! He's in the pass, waiting for you. . . ."

Tim jumped down beside Grant. "How do you know this?" he demanded. "Who sent you?"

"Sent myself. Matt Cord! Judas goat! He's in with Red Feather! Wagon train this spring. Same thing. Hurry . . . no time!"

"You heard him," Winslow said, picking up the almost weightless bag of bones and flinging him onto Tim's saddle. "Get him back to your wagon. Now! And spread the alarm!" Winslow quickly looked around and spotted a ridge a half mile to the west with a stand of aspen running along its spine. He pointed to it. "Tell the wagons to head for that ridge, and not to worry about staying in a line. Now git! I'll catch up with you."

Tim swung up behind his saddle and with one arm around Grant, spurred his horse back to the wagon train.

By the time Winslow had climbed back up onto the stagecoach beside Throckmorton, the wagons already had broken for the ridge. He swung his horses around, cracked his bullwhip over their heaving backs, and lifted them to a pounding gallop that soon brought him abreast the long line of wagons. In a moment he had pulled ahead and was well out in front when he heard Throckmorton yell in his ear to look to his right.

Winslow did and saw Red Feather's band pouring out of the pass, their ponies strung out in a long line as they tried desperately to cut off the wagons before they reached the ridge.

After a few moments, Winslow found himself in rifle range of the nearest Indian. Without hesitation, he thrust the reins into Throckmorton's hands and snatched up his Sharps. Leading the Indian carefully, he squeezed off a shot. The Indian peeled back off his pony, and Throckmorton let out a yell of triumph that could have been heard in the last ring of Hades.

Snatching back the reins, Winslow handed Throckmorton the rifle.

"Reload it," he told the doctor.

"I can't."

"Well, you'd better learn. And damn soon!"

"I have a feeling I will."

The racing file of Indians was strung out behind the stage now as Winslow continued to pull rapidly ahead. To his left, the wagons were managing to keep up, the drivers having increased their pace considerably the moment they sighted the Indians. They probably hadn't really believed it when Tim raced back and told them to head for the ridge, but they sure as hell were believers now.

The stage tipped precariously as the team plunged up the steep slope to the top of the ridge. For a second or two Winslow was afraid he had asked too much of the horses and the coach, but the moment passed and the horses gained the ridge. The stagecoach, rocking dangerously, followed after. The wagons took a more circuitous route to the top of the ridge, and Winslow noticed the Indians had held up for a moment, assessing the situation. He took the opportunity to climb down from his box and empty the stage of its terrified passengers. He told Throckmorton to escort Kate and the girls out of danger behind the crest of the ridge, where they were to wait for the arrival of the wagons.

Swiftly reloading his rifle, he found a spot among the rocks that gave him a clear line of fire at the Indians, who now were closing slowly upon the ridge. He took his time and dropped two more warriors before the others turned and began racing broadside along the ridge, brandishing their rifles and ki-yiing furiously.

This was fine with Winslow. While they were busy showing off their horsemanship below, the wagons were reaching the ridge from behind him, and it was not long before men were pouring down into the rocks to join him. Joshua Beechwood had a Hawken rifle and a steady hand. He barely had slumped down beside Winslow before he caught one brave in the neck and spilled him back into the tall grass.

Soon after, Red Feather pulled his warriors out of range for a parley. Winslow had a good idea they were not going to vote to pull out this soon, but probably they already had lost more of their number than they had planned on losing. He had caught sight of Red Feather early on. The half-breed was, after all, the tallest Indian and the only one flaunting a red feather. It was clear now that Thomas Grant had spoken the truth. Matt Cord not only had advised Red Feather of this wagon train's route, he undoubtedly had done the same thing with the wagon train that had been wiped out earlier.

Winslow got to his feet and looked around. Beyond the stagecoach, high on the ridge, the wagons had been drawn into a tight circle by the women, with the stock inside. The women were in there also, and occasionally he could see bonneted faces peering out through the wheel spokes.

Leaving Tim Curry in charge, Winslow climbed up into the stagecoach's box and drove it up the slope and into the wagon train circle. As he unharnessed the team, he explained the situation to Throckmorton and the women, trying to be as optimistic as he realistically could. When he left to return to his men, he was confident the women wouldn't panic. They seemed to have genuine faith in his and the other men's ability to stop Red Feather.

Returning to the rocks, he looked over his troops. Tim Curry was on his left, and beyond him were Phil Turner and Bill Walsh. All that Walsh had to fight with was a huge Walker Colt revolver, but it would have to do—and undoubtedly would come in quite handy in close combat. Deacon Smathers was on his right, just on the other side of Beechwood. The deacon held a battered, nondescript rifle and had a revolver stuck in his belt. Winslow hoped the cleric was capable of using them. Beyond Smathers crouched Noah Whittington. The rifle Noah was brandishing looked like a Kentucky long rifle, and if so, these Indians were in trouble. Noah caught Winslow's eye and winked. The old man must have been in his early seventies at least, but he obviously was enjoying himself greatly.

The only man not among them was Braden Throckmorton, who was back among the wagons doing his best to see to the needs of Thomas Grant. And that was fine with Winslow. The good doctor's services undoubtedly would be needed later on, and there was no sense in exposing him unnecessarily.

"They've stopped their palaver," Beechwood drawled.

Looking back at Red Feather and his band, Winslow saw the Indians riding away from the ridge. As soon as their ponies were well out of range, they dismounted and spread out on foot. Using the tall grass as cover, they ducked low and were soon out of sight. Only an occasional movement betrayed their presence as they crept closer to the ridge.

"They'll be coming at us from all sides now,"

Beechwood commented softly. "From the other side of this ridge as well."

Winslow nodded. "Take a couple of men and cover our rear," Winslow told him. "I figure they'll make one more push around dusk. You shouldn't have any trouble stopping them. But when it gets dark, delay them as long as you can, then break back to the wagons. We'll be doing the same thing. Those who get there first will cover the others."

Beechwood nodded, then moved swiftly down the line, tapping Bill Walsh and Phil Turner as he went. In a moment the trio had vanished over the ridge and into the aspen.

Tim Curry moved closer. "I heard what you told Joshua," he said. "You think they'll still come after us in the dark?"

"That's what I'm thinking."

"But I thought Indians never attacked at night."

Winslow laughed.

Noah Whittington piped up then. "In that case, Tim, as soon as it gets dark you go right to sleep. We'll wake you come morning." He spat. "Maybe."

"I read that somewhere," Tim admitted ruefully. "I suppose it's a pretty silly idea at that, ain't it?"

"It sure as hell is," Winslow replied. "The Indian does most of his fighting by the light of the moon when there is one—and in pitch dark when the moon's missing."

"I can't see a single aborigine," complained Smathers. He lifted his head to view the meadow below them from a higher angle. A shot from a clump of grass less than twenty yards away sent a ricocheting slug off a rock face inches from the deacon's head. He ducked down as if he had been shot.

"Maybe you can't see them, Deacon," Noah drawled, "but they sure as hell can see you. The next time you stick

111

your head up like that, you'll get it turned inside out. That redskin's got your range now.''

Smathers shrank still lower, his face chalk white.

''I think it's time we spread out among these rocks,'' Winslow said. ''But keep down. Noah's right—those Indians have our range now, and they are excellent marksmen.''

The men moved out, keeping as low as possible. In a moment they were out of sight—all except Tim Curry, who found a nice vantage spot in a nest of boulders to Winslow's left. Winslow made himself as comfortable as he could behind a boulder—and waited.

Tim Curry was worried. Not about himself, but about Samantha. And though he found it embarrassing to admit, he was concerned about Terry Lambert as well. He glanced over at Winslow.

''I'm ducking back to the wagons,'' he called softly. ''I want to check on Samantha and the others. It won't take long.''

''Good idea,'' said Scott, just as softly. ''Go ahead. I'll cover for you.''

Keeping low and doing his best not to favor his weak leg, Tim reached the wagon train without incident and ducked between his wagon and Noah's. Glancing into his own wagon, he saw Samantha in her rocker. The wagon shook rhythmically as the tall woman rocked. Both her hands were riveted to the rocker's arms, and her eyes were wide and staring.

Tim didn't like what he saw. ''You all right, Samantha?'' he inquired anxiously, aware even as he asked the question how foolish it was.

''Be careful, Tim,'' the woman managed. ''Be careful! Take your knife! Cut them! Slice out their black hearts!''

''Yes, Samantha,'' Tim responded, wincing. ''I'll be

careful. And you'll be all right in here. But try and stay down. Maybe you shouldn't sit in your rocker.''

"Be careful,'' she repeated. "Take your knife!''

It was frustrating as hell for Tim to listen to her when she was like this. He knew she was half out of her mind, now that the threat of an Indian attack had become a reality. His only hope was that if they managed to defeat Red Feather, Samantha would realize the Indians weren't invincible—that they could be stopped. Perhaps then she might banish once and for all the ghosts that tore at her mind.

He turned from the wagon and was about to return to the rocks when he caught sight of Terry standing beside the stagecoach. She had seen him enter the ring of wagons and was watching him now, hoping that he would notice her.

Tim waved, and Terry came running. "Oh, Tim,'' she cried. "I'm so frightened! This is all so terrifying! I never realized before how awful it would be.''

"Calm down, Terry,'' he said, reaching out and taking her by the shoulders. "We're well armed, and Scott's handling things nicely. As long as the savages keep trying frontal attacks, we have the advantage.''

"Do you think they'll . . .'' She paused at the enormity of what she was thinking. "Do you think they might even break through to the wagons?''

"It's a possibility,'' he told her honestly. "But I don't think they will.''

She shuddered. "I read once where the men always gave a woman a loaded gun . . . to use, just in case.'' She looked with terrified eyes at Tim. "But I have nothing.''

"Forget about guns. They're not going to get through.''

"But . . . suppose they do?''

"Here,'' Tim said, slipping his hunting knife from its

sheath. "If they come near you, use this. Think about living, Terry. Not dying."

She took the knife. "It's so big," she said.

"Is it too big? Can you handle it?"

She closed her right hand firmly around the handle, then looked up at Tim, a grim and determined look on her face. "I can handle it," she told him.

"Good," he said. "But don't worry. We won't let them through."

Impulsively, Terry raised herself on tiptoe and kissed Tim on the lips. Before he could respond, she turned and raced back to the stagecoach, then turned back to him and waved.

Tim returned her wave, and with his head spinning slightly, he hurried from the wagons to rejoin Scott and the others. He had a promise to keep, and he sure as hell was determined to keep it.

Chapter 9

As Scott Winslow expected, the next attack came at dusk. It was a foolish move by an overanxious brave determined to gain renown. He rose out of the grass, firing as he came, and dashed toward the settlers. He got as far as the rocks before Winslow fired carefully, planting a black hole in his chest. But somehow the warrior kept coming.

As swiftly as he could, but with infinite care, Winslow reloaded. The brave was almost on him when he swung up his barrel and fired. The round singed the Indian's flesh just under his rib cage. It was as good as a miss. Winslow dropped his rifle and was reaching for his Colt when Tim Curry shot the brave in the back.

As the Indian toppled into his lap, Winslow saw Tim swiftly lever his rifle and swing it around just in time to pick off another Indian rushing at them from a cleft in the rocks. All along the line now, Winslow heard the sudden crackle of rifle fire. The firing lasted for no more than a couple of minutes, however. As quickly as it began, the attack ended.

Winslow took the opportunity to check with all the defenders on his side. Not a man had been hit. But as he returned to his position, he heard the sound of gunfire coming from the other side of the aspen. He left the rocks and slipped over the ridge, coming out of the trees just behind Joshua Beechwood. The fellow had his Hawken trained on Winslow as he broke into the clear.

"Better whistle next time," said Beechwood, lowering his rifle. "I had an idea it might be you coming. But I was ready, just in case."

"I heard shooting."

"Yes. We caught a few of the bastards, and the rest fell back. But they're still down there in the rocks, waiting for dark. I can smell them."

"Anyone hurt?"

"Nope. Phil Turner's over there below that clump of juniper. He accounted for one of them. He's a real cool customer—waited until the redskin was on top of him before he blasted the sonofabitch. Said he wanted to make sure."

"How's Bill Walsh doing?"

"He knocked one of them on his ass with that little cannon of his. I hope it helps him stop shaking."

A fleeting grin passed over Winslow's face. He didn't need to ask how Beechwood himself was doing. "You're right. They'll be back, come dark," he told Joshua. "Get as many as you can, but don't delay pulling back to the wagons."

"I heard you the first time," Beechwood said grimly.

Satisfied, Winslow left to check on the wagons.

Kate was the first to approach when he slipped in through the wagons. To his surprise, she was holding a gleaming hunting rifle.

"Where in hell did you get that beauty, Kate?" he asked quickly.

"I'll tell you if you'll let me use it."

"Can you shoot it?"

"I can."

He took the rifle and examined it carefully. Despite its large caliber, it was astonishingly light—a breech-loading Remington, skillfully cut down for her use. The workmanship was excellent throughout.

"Nice balance," he commented, hefting it.

"Careful," she said. "I've already loaded it."

He handed it back and waited for her explanation. Smiling slightly, she said, "I had a gentleman friend in Denver who liked to take me shooting. Sometimes, he actually found time to show me how to use it. He said I was an apt pupil."

"This is warfare, Kate. To the death. Those savages down there mean to kill you—but not until after they've had their amusement. But if you think you can shoot well enough, fine. Stay up here and give us cover when we break back to these wagons later."

He looked around then at the women peering nervously at him. The looks on their faces revealed the terror they were trying to control. It was obvious they no longer were as confident as they had been when the battle began. Poor Collette La Tour was nowhere in sight, but Winslow could hear her clearly. She was huddled inside the stage, weeping.

Glancing back at Kate, he asked, "Is Throckmorton still with Grant?"

Kate nodded. "Yes. That poor crazed man's still yammering nonstop and doing an inspired job of unnerving a lot of us. I don't think he'll be much good if those savages break through."

"He's already saved our lives," Winslow reminded her. "Do what you can to help the doctor. We may need him later."

"You sound as if you're expecting *me* to take charge here."

"That's exactly what I'm expecting, Kate. Tell the women it's all right. So far, we've been able to handle Red Feather, even killed a few of his number. Encourage them. Some of them have weapons, I see. Do what you can to prevent them from shooting any of us when we fall back to the wagons later."

She nodded quickly, evidently pleased he was placing such trust in her.

"And yes, Kate," he said, smiling at her with sudden warmth. "You may shoot that Remington if you wish. That's what it was built for, I understand."

There was no further move from Red Feather's forces until dark. Fortunately, the moon—a bright, harvest moon—was out almost immediately, gleaming in the heavens like a newly minted silver dollar. Its light helped the defenders a great deal.

Two braves led the assault on Winslow's position. He stopped one with his Sharps, then resorted to his Colt, catching the second one high in the chest and slamming him back down among the rocks. As he reloaded his Sharps, he saw Tim picking off Indians as calmly as a farmer at a turkey shoot. Tim's rate of fire impressed Winslow greatly, as did his remarkable accuracy. The Henry repeater was a fine weapon, but the young soldier behind it, Winslow realized, had just as much quality.

It was the devastating toll of Tim's rapid and accurate fire that caused this third assault to fail. Once again, Red Feather's braves vanished into the grass. The next wait was a long one—deliberately so, Winslow had no doubt.

It was midnight when he heard the heel of a moccasin strike the surface of a rock behind him. Swinging his Colt around, he fired up at the figure hurtling at him through the darkness. The sweating body struck him a numbing blow, but when Winslow flung the brave off him, the Indian rolled lifelessly into the rocks below.

Just then another brave leaped out of the night at him. There was no time for Winslow to fire. He unsheathed his hunting knife a second before the Indian struck him. With his left forearm, he warded off his attacker's war hatchet. And with his right, he drove the hunting knife deep into the man's chest. He heard the brave gasp. As Winslow withdrew his weapon, he felt the sudden warm gush of blood that followed it. The blood drenched his shirt and britches, but Winslow ignored it as he caught sight of a brave advancing on Tim from behind. Tim was busy firing at a host of warriors coming at him from the rocks below, and didn't see his attacker.

"Tim!" Winslow cried, as he swung up his Sharps.

Tim whirled around just as Winslow fired. The Indian jackknifed, then tumbled past Tim's position, bowling into another brave climbing up from below.

"Move back!" Winslow cried to Tim as he holstered his Colt and sheathed his knife. "To the wagons!"

At once, Tim and the others left their positions and dashed up the slope, firing behind them as they went. As they neared the wagons, ragged fire from inside the circle did much to discourage what remained of Red Feather's band. One rifle in particular seemed effective—Kate's Remington.

A moment later Scott's group was providing cover for Beechwood and the others as they, too, retreated to the protection of the wagons. The battle raged for almost an hour longer. Only a few of Red Feather's braves managed to get through the barrier, and these were disposed of with relative ease by the defenders, usually with sidearms at close range. Bill Walsh's big Walker Colt came in especially handy.

A few hours before dawn, Red Feather tried to burn out the settlers. But Winslow had alerted the women, and buckets of water were ready beside each wagon. The first burning arrow that lodged in the canvas of one of the wagons was ripped out and tossed to the ground by a furious Mary Turner. Another flaming arrow set fire to the canvas covering the deacon's wagon, but the bucket brigade swiftly doused the flames.

After that attempt, the night grew quiet—too quiet. Near dawn, Terry Lambert began screaming. The sound sent the hair standing straight up on the back of Winslow's neck. It was a terrible, piercing scream—the cry of a woman in flight from all the fiends of hell.

Kate Harrow was the first to reach the stagecoach and found Terry lying face up on the ground beside it, an Indian on top of her. With the butt of her Remington, Kate struck the Indian a vicious blow on the side of his head, sending him flopping off the still-screaming girl. She could immediately see that the Indian was dead, but that it wasn't her own blow that had killed him. The hilt of Tim Curry's hunting knife protruded from the dead man's breast, where Terry had plunged it when the brave tried to carry her away.

Averting her eyes from the dead Indian, Kate fought back her nausea and knelt by Terry, who continued to scream hysterically. Kate slapped her, twice. Shocked into silence, Terry looked with sudden comprehension into Kate's eyes, then began to cry softly. Lifting Terry gently in her arms, Kate carried her into the protection of the stagecoach—Throckmorton and Tim Curry crowding in after her. As Throckmorton examined the distraught girl, Collette stopped her interminable weeping—and proceeded to wail uncontrollably instead.

From outside the stage, Winslow heard a sharp slap.

Then Collette, too, was silent. Winslow poked his head into the coach.

"I hated to do it," Kate told him. "But I've had enough of Collette's foolishness."

"How's Terry?" Winslow asked.

"There's a nasty bump on her head, but she'll be all right. She's just scared silly, is all. I'll let Tim calm her, if you can spare him."

Winslow nodded and then went back to the others to take stock. The only casualties were minor. Beechwood had warded off a blade with his forearm. The slash was deep, but apparently nothing vital had been severed, and the doctor had already cleaned out the wound and bound it securely. Bill Walsh had a flesh wound in his right calf, which he had cleaned and bandaged himself.

The rest suffered mostly from nerves and a lack of sleep. Noah Whittington was almost totally exhausted, Winslow noted, and Ruth was out of her sick bed and fluttering anxiously around him. Phil Turner was sitting close by his young wife, who was silent and vigilant. The two suddenly seemed very close and content.

It was Deacon Smathers who surprised Winslow the most, however. Before the action he had appeared timid, frightened. But he was a mouse no longer. Indeed, he appeared altogether exhilarated by the experience—perhaps too much so, Winslow thought as he watched the man peering out into the night, his eyes lit with excitement, his hands trembling eagerly as they held his rifle. For the first time, Winslow glimpsed a new and much less amiable person behind those wire spectacles.

As soon as dawn broke, Scott Winslow and Tim Curry moved back down among the rocks. What they saw was heartening. A small cluster of braves had gathered around Red Feather, while a single brave was seen walking away from them toward the horses grazing in the distance.

Red Feather's band had shrunk noticeably since the engagement began the afternoon before. At least half of his force was missing, and now there was a good chance the rest would soon pull out. Because of Grant's timely warning, any chance Red Feather had of a quick massacre was long gone.

Back at the circle of wagons, Samantha Ridley slowly and cautiously climbed out of Tim's wagon. Once on the ground, she glanced furtively around her. Bent slightly over, she turned her back on Mary Turner and Amanda Beechwood, who were conversing softly in front of the next wagon, then moved slyly to the rear of Tim's wagon and reached in.

From a tool chest, she pulled a huge carving knife and tucked it into the heavy folds of her skirt. She turned around then and looked up at the sky. It was dawn. A new day. She could hear birds chirping in the aspen behind the wagons. But it was not joyous life that had burst in on her—but that same old horror. Once again she had heard her little girl scream—and in that instant had known what she must do.

The savages had returned. She had rocked and rocked, but still they came at her, their hideous faces pushing close, their bloody hatchets dripping. At first she had thought her little girl was safe and had eluded her pursuers in the dark. But then the little angel had stopped screaming, and her tiny form had been flung down upon the boards of the wagon. Looking down, Samantha had seen her daughter's lifeless body, her blond curls smeared with blood.

And now those same demons waited for her. Though they were quiet now, she was not deceived. Fiends out of hell, they were out there now, hatchets dripping.

She slipped past the rear of Tim's wagon and peered

122

craftily toward the rocks and the grassland beyond. Yes! She saw the painted devils!

"Samantha! Is anything wrong?"

Samantha whirled to see Kate Harrow reaching out toward her.

Pulling violently away from Kate's reaching hand, Samantha spun back around, and with a fierce wail—wrung from the depths of her tormented soul—she charged out through the wagons and raced down the slope, her long legs carrying her over the uneven ground with astonishing speed.

At the sound of a woman's scream, Winslow turned in time to see Samantha, a huge carving knife in her hand, running swiftly down the slope toward them. At the same time, racing after her, Kate broke from the wagons.

"Stop her!" Kate cried. "She's gone mad!"

Winslow didn't need Kate's explanation to understand Samantha's insane purpose. He and Tim jumped to their feet and raced up the ridge toward her. Tim reached her first, but was flung violently aside by the demented woman. Her face contorted, she slashed at Winslow, then dodged nimbly past him and fled down the rocks with remarkable agility.

In a moment she had reached the grassland. As Winslow and Tim raced frantically after her, she bolted swiftly through the grass toward the astonished Indians, who were just about to mount their horses. Before Red Feather and his braves could recover from their surprise, she was among them, slashing and screaming. The Indians cried out in honest terror as they scattered before her. More than one of them was caught by Samantha's flashing knife as she raged among them with the force and fury of a hurricane.

But Red Feather was not intimidated. As the others mounted up and fled, he stepped in close, parried one of

Samantha's knife thrusts with his rifle, then swung the weapon like a club. It caught Samantha on the side of her head, staggering her. But she didn't go down. With a soul-curdling yell, she plunged toward the half-breed. Red Feather ducked almost casually to one side and discharged his rifle into her stomach. Then seeing Winslow and Tim racing toward him, he swiftly mounted up and rode after the rest of his band.

Behind him, Samantha dropped lifeless to the grass, smiling, at peace, the fierce war chants no longer tormenting her soul.

Samantha Ridley was buried on the ridge. Deacon Smathers spoke eloquently over her grave, recounting her awesome tribulations and assuring everyone that a terrible but just God not only would understand and forgive her transgressions, but would welcome her with gladness into Paradise. There at last, in perfect peace and contentment, she would be reunited with her husband and child.

But it was Tim, profoundly saddened by Samantha's death, who made the most moving statement of all. As the wagons pulled out off the ridge, he remained by her gravesite and played for Samantha her favorite hymn, "Nearer My God to Thee."

As the harmonica's haunting notes drifted off the ridge to where Scott Winslow was seated atop the stagecoach, he felt a deep, aching emptiness—something he had felt only once before, at the funeral of his father.

Beside him, Braden Throckmorton stared blankly ahead, doing his best to ignore the tears that coursed down his cheeks. Pretending not to notice the tears, Winslow took the doctor's offered flask gladly and without comment.

Chapter 10

Before entering Deadman's Pass, Winslow halted the wagon train, saddled one of the horses, and scouted the pass thoroughly. Satisfied that Red Feather had given up on them and departed to lick his considerable wounds, Winslow climbed back up onto the stagecoach and led the wagon train into the pass.

They were almost through it when he heard the doctor's gasp. Winslow turned. Throckmorton's face had gone as white as a frog's belly as he stared up at a pine on the ridge above them. Following Throckmorton's stunned gaze, Winslow quickly found himself hoping that no one below would be unfortunate enough to glance out of the stagecoach window at that moment.

Matt Cord, twisting slowly in the wind, was hanging at the end of a thick rawhide lariat, with his hands bound tightly behind his back. Winslow knew it was Matt Cord because of the slack, chinless face. No scalp remained, and there was little else to identify the former wagon master. Ragged, bloody strips of skin hung from his flailed corpse. Portions of his ribs and backbone gleamed whitely in the morning sun. In the bright blue sky high above, like cinders caught in an updraft, vultures wheeled uncertainly, deciding how best to digest this meal.

For the first time in his life, Winslow knew for sure what *skinned alive* meant.

The first emotion Winslow felt was horror. Then came relief, as though a burden with the weight of an anvil had been lifted from his shoulders . . . and from his soul. Red Feather had done what he had been reluctant to do for himself. Matt Cord, the man who murdered his father, was dead. But after the relief washed through him, Winslow felt a sudden emptiness—as if all direction had been taken from him. He felt suddenly adrift. Purposeless.

A sudden cry of terror came from one of the wagons behind him. It sounded like Amanda Beechwood. Almost immediately thereafter came Grant's high, gibbering laughter as he, too, caught sight of Red Feather's handiwork. Cursing violently, Winslow snatched up his whip and sent it cracking over the backs of his horses, lifting them to a sudden gallop, a pace he maintained until the stage was well clear of the pass.

When he finally slowed the team down, an obviously troubled Kate called up to him. "What's wrong? What was that scream, Scott?"

"Later!" Winslow shouted down. His tone was warning enough, and she didn't ask any more questions.

A few minutes later, he glanced behind him and saw that all the wagons had cleared the pass. Now they were moving onto a gently swelling parkland that took them steadily higher. Winslow relaxed and glanced over at the still-shaken doctor.

"A man who follows my calling shouldn't be affected by such things, I suppose," Throckmorton managed, as he dabbed at his forehead with his handkerchief. "But you must admit—that was a most disconcerting sight, indeed."

"It was worse than that, Doctor," Winslow told him grimly. "When I scouted that pass earlier, take my word for it—Matt Cord had not yet been hung out to dry. I guess I underestimated Red Feather. He and the rest of his pack haven't given up on us at all."

"You mean . . . ?"

"That's right. And what you saw back there was his way of letting us know."

As the day wore on, a cold rain began to fall. Ahead of him, Winslow saw black glowering clouds rolling in from the west, completely blotting out the sun. As the trail continued to lift them toward the now-driving rain, it suddenly turned to snow, which began to accumulate with incredible swiftness. Before long the entire wagon train was moving through a snow squall so fierce that at times Winslow had difficulty seeing his lead horse. He managed to keep going, however, as occasional breaks in the shifting clouds enabled him to catch a glimpse of the parkland over which they were traveling.

The snow grew deeper. Throckmorton shivered under his cloak, and Winslow's slicker became heavy with the accumulation. Winslow found himself squinting continually as the sleetlike snow lashed at his face and stung his eyes.

"We'd better stop!" the doctor cried as night fell. "We can't go any farther tonight."

"No!" Winslow told him. "We keep going. If we get caught on this ridge tonight, we'll never survive. We've got to keep going until we find some protection."

"But how can we go on?" Throckmorton demanded, as he glanced around in a panic. "I can't see any of the wagons. We've left them behind."

"They'll follow our tracks, damn you!" Winslow

cried above the screaming wind. "Now stop bellyaching and break out that whiskey!"

Somewhat chastened, Throckmorton dug into his black bag and managed to pull the flask from it. After first taking a generous swig himself, he handed the flask to Winslow, who drank deeply.

The fiery liquid did little for Winslow's morale. He wasn't nearly as sure of himself as he wanted Throckmorton to believe. But one thing he did know—this exposed ridge was no place for them to stop now. If they did, the snow would soon bury them alive. For the rest of this fall and on through winter, he knew, the snowfall at this altitude would be almost constant, with the depth reaching as much as thirty or more feet before the spring thaws commenced.

They had no choice. They *had* to keep going.

The night became a howling, Stygian darkness—but still Winslow kept going. The swirling snow tore at his face and eyes. His cheekbones and nose stung with a touch of frostbite, and his hands were getting numb, but he refused to lose heart. As the snow flew at him straight on, the land continued to rise—which meant they were still heading due west and weren't lost. The itinerary Smathers had shown Winslow before they entered the pass had described this portion of the trail as a steady incline due west until the divide was reached. The trail supposedly was four miles in length, with plenty of grass and some water. But there had been no mention of wood, which was easy to understand. They now were well above the timber line.

There no longer were any complaints from Throckmorton, for Winslow had stopped long enough to enable the nearly frozen doctor to climb down and take refuge in the coach. Now, as he glanced back through the shifting curtains of snow, Winslow caught a glimpse of the wagons still following him. If they kept up and managed to stay in his tracks, they wouldn't get lost. But if any of them lagged behind, the wind would obliterate the tracks of the wagons in front, and they and the wagons behind them would wander off across the plateau, lost in a white, frozen hell.

Winslow prayed that this wouldn't happen.

Suddenly the ground beneath the stage leveled off. Winslow felt it at once. Then the trail began to drop, ever so slightly, and the horses appeared to be laboring less. Winslow had reached the divide and now was passing over it. Soon, he hoped, they would reach the tree line and leave the worst of the storm behind them.

But it was not as soon as Winslow hoped. For at least three miserable hours longer, he drove his exhausted, stumbling team on. Now, at least, the wind and driving snow had shifted to his back, the flakes gentler. Occasionally he saw rifts in the clouds and caught glimpses of stars winking high overhead.

They finally reached the timber as the snowfall continued to abate. Visibility improved markedly, and a clear moon suddenly shone through, lighting the snow-covered landscape. Catching sight of a benchland under a sheltering ridge, Winslow directed his horses off the trail toward it. A few minutes later he reined in the team. His frozen bones creaking, he climbed down from his icy perch, searching the trail behind him for the wagons. He caught sight of two wagons heading for the benchland after him. Alarmed, he wondered if they were all who had made it.

As it turned out, Winslow needn't have worried. Each wagon eventually arrived on the benchland, with Candy and Bill Walsh being the last to show up, just before dawn. Two more-frightened pilgrims Winslow had never seen. They had kept on doggedly—half-mad with the cold and barely able to see the trail ahead of them—but they hadn't given up, and thus had made it.

For the next three days the snow continued to fall, at times nearly a blizzard. At night the winds howled around the wagons, whipping the snow into fantastic, impassable drifts. But the sheltering ridge kept them free of the worst blasts, as the circle of wagons turned into a kind of snow-city, with warm fires and even some laughter as the shut-ins rested and waited.

Melody Tinsdale stretched like a large cat and smiled up at Joshua, her arms still around his neck.

"Mmm," she murmured, her voice silky with contentment. "You shouldn't worry, Joshua. You're still plenty of man for a girl like me."

Joshua knew Melody was supposed to say this sort of thing. It was part of Kate Harrow's training, and it made good sense. There were few men foolish enough to complain upon hearing such a pronouncement.

Fortunately, Joshua knew his talents were such that a woman could say this and mean it.

Melody began to nibble on his earlobe. He chuckled softly and snuggled closer to her warmth, his big hand closing around one of her breasts. Laughing softly, delightedly, Melody's lips left his ear, dropped to his neck, and then began nibbling on the white, wiry hair of his chest.

"Where you going?" he asked drowsily, as her lips moved still farther down his chest.

"Collette ain't the only girl with talent around here," Melody told him.

He didn't stop her. Closing his eyes, he rolled over onto his back, his senses reeling. All awareness of time faded. The snow and the cold and the trip still ahead belonged to another time, another world. All that mattered now was this tent and this woman and what she was doing for him. . . .

*   *   *

Dressed, Joshua Beechwood peeked out of the tent. The coast was clear. Turning back, he kissed Melody. Mischievously, she nipped his lower lip, then pushed him out into the sudden cold. He stumbled through the darkness—it was as if he was drunk, he realized. He felt impossibly empty, as light as a feather. A crushing, sick burden had been lifted from his soul—no, purged from his entrails. He was less than he had been when first he entered Melody's tent—and more, so much more.

As he climbed into his wagon, he heard Amanda stir and sit up. While he began the clumsy business of undressing, she struck a sulfur match and lit the lantern. In its flickering glow he saw her pinched, hard face and her cold, angry eyes. He almost laughed aloud. What did it matter what Amanda felt or cared or said? What did any of that matter now?

He could tell she sensed his defiant lack of concern. She knew as he did that they had crossed over a line. There wasn't anything she could do or say any longer to pleasure him or to hurt him. She had withheld herself from him for the last time. Each of them was no longer responsible for the happiness, or the unhappiness, of the other.

Inexplicably, this thought saddened Joshua, but he shook it off as he slid his long body under the sheets.

"You going to keep that lantern on all night?" he muttered as he turned his face to the canvas.

"I know where you were," Amanda said, her voice surprisingly soft.

He turned his head to look at her. "So?"

"I just wanted you to know. And I understand."

Joshua turned completely over and looked at his wife. Tears were coursing down her cheeks. He was astounded—as much by her tears as by the effect they had on him.

"What do you mean, you understand?" he asked.

"Do I have to explain?"

"Yes, woman. You do."

"She is younger and prettier than I am. I no longer . . . appeal to you."

"Hogwash, and you know it. That's got nothing at all to do with it. And you know that, too."

He was being brutally honest with her, but he sensed there was no other way now. And besides, what did it matter if he no longer was gentle? The time for gentleness and sweet consideration had long since passed.

She wiped her tears away with the back of her knuckles and frowned. "Then it's something else?"

"I'm a man, and there are times when I need a woman. If you won't have me, then I must—and I will—find someone who will. I'm not dead yet. And those women who sleep with me are perfectly willing to admit that fact."

"Are you sorry you came back to me?"

"Yes."

"You miss Annabel?"

"Very much."

"You loved her?"

"Yes."

"But you came back to me."

"Is that so strange? I thought you needed me. You said you did. And I still loved you."

"So that's why you returned to me?" Her voice was small with wonder.

"Yes."

"But I didn't let you love me, and Annabel did."

"Yes, she did," he openly admitted to her. "And she loved me in return."

"And now this . . . girl of Kate Harrow's. Does she love you?"

"As far as she is able. She is only a girl. And a

132

whore. But for a while—a brief while—she allows me to think that she loves me. It is a pleasant enough game, if that is all one has."

"And that's all you have?"

"For now. Yes."

She looked at him for a long moment, and it seemed to Joshua that she could see into his very soul. If she could, she would know he was speaking the truth. It was too late now to hide anything.

Amanda turned her face from his. This time her tears came in a steady flow, and she made no effort to wipe them away. Through the tears, she said, "I have been so stupid. So cruel. You're only a man."

"And you're a woman." To Joshua's amazement, there were tears in his eyes as well. "And you could have been my woman. It's what I've always wanted—what I've waited all these years for."

"Is it too late now?" she asked, looking back at him, seeing for the first time the tears on his cheeks.

"Yes."

"Damn you! It is *not* too late."

"Prove it."

"I will." She reached for him.

"No. Not now, Amanda," he said, pulling the covers up over his shoulder and turning his face to the canvas. "Let me think on this awhile. We've had a remarkable conversation. But it's late." He paused, and a delicious memory shuddered through him. "And I've had a busy night."

Amanda turned off the lantern, then wiped her eyes and pulled the covers over her shoulders. She turned to Joshua, but he was asleep already. Slowly, deliberately, she eased her body against his and closed her eyes.

She, too, was filled with wonder at the conversation they had just had. How incredibly simple everything was finally—for the unalterable truth was that each loved the other. So now all that remained was for her to show him how much she loved him. And she *would* show him. Content with that thought, Amanda slept.

On the fourth day, the sun came up on a dazzlingly white landscape. The sky was crisp and clear. An air of festivity swept through the wagon party. The only jarring note was Ruth Whittington's incessant coughing, which had grown steadily worse despite Dr. Throckmorton's efforts to ease it. But everyone—including Noah—believed that Ruth would surely get better as soon as they reached the Willamette Valley. And the valley was but a few days away.

A heady optimism filled the settlers as they began harnessing their horses and repacking the wagons. But Scott Winslow knew that nothing was ever as simple as it appeared on the surface, and so he had sent Tim earlier that morning to scout back along the trail toward the pass. He hadn't forgotten the threat implied in that ribboned corpse Red Feather had planted in the sky.

The wagons were about ready to pull out when Tim returned. Watching Tim's gray plunging through the heavy drifts, its legs sending geysers of snow up past its haunches, Winslow knew something was up. He left off harnessing the stage team and labored through the hip-deep snow to meet Tim.

The young man leaped from his mount and plunged through the drifts to Winslow's side. He was breathing hard, and his face was beet red from windburn. "I saw signs," he said.

"Red Feather?"

"Looks like it. It's about the right size party, and the tracks were coming from the pass."

"He's a persistent devil."

"What do you think we should do?"

"Get the hell out of here. I've already harnessed your team, and Grant has secured your wagon. Hurry up. We're pulling out now."

Nodding briskly, Tim led his mount past Winslow, who swiftly finished harnessing his horses and climbed up beside an anxious Throckmorton.

"What's up?" the doctor asked. He had witnessed Winslow's hurried conversation with Tim and didn't miss the concern on Winslow's face as he clambered up beside him.

"Tim's seen Indian signs. Hostiles, more'n likely."

"You mean Red Feather?"

Winslow released the brake lever and sent his whip crackling out over his team. "Yup."

"He's a persistent devil."

"You took the words right out of my mouth."

By noon that day they had left the heavy drifts behind as they traveled steadily downhill. On ground barely dusted with snow, they camped that night with pickets on guard, the men spelling each other at four-hour intervals. The following night they found a frozen patch of meadow beside an icy mountain stream. They weren't yet out of the chill grasp of the mountains, but already there was more than a hint of the temperate valley toward which they were riding.

By now, however, everyone in the wagon train knew that Ruth Whittington was dying.

"Braden!" Kate called, as she hurried from the stage to intercept the doctor.

"What is it, Kate?" Throckmorton asked as he turned to face her.

"The girls and I are worried about Ruth," she ex-

135

plained as she took his arm and led him to a quiet spot behind the stage. "Isn't there anything you can do?"

Sighing wearily, Throckmorton shook his head with sad finality. "I have done all I can. My entire pharmacopoeia is at her disposal. But the prognosis, I am afraid, is not good."

"What is it? What's wrong? She hasn't coughed all day. We thought she was getting better."

The doctor's smile was ironic. "She is too weak to cough. Her lungs are congested, raw with inflammation. If only she could cough, she might be able to throw off that which is drowning her." Throckmorton took Kate gently by the hand. "Kate, she has the pneumonia."

"Oh, my God," she whispered.

"Yes, Kate," the doctor said, nodding his head slightly. "She is in God's hands now."

"But . . . you must do something, Braden. Anything to ease her."

"I have exhausted my quinine and have only a little opium left. Perhaps the opium would ease her, though she hasn't complained of pain since yesterday."

"Do what you can, Braden," Kate said softly. "Please. I would feel so much better."

"As you say, Kate."

A moment later, his black bag in hand, Throckmorton stepped up into the Whittingtons's wagon and thrust his shoulders inside. Noah was crouched at the far end of the wagon, with Ruth in her bed beside him. Their hands were clasped together.

Throckmorton, his cumbersome bulk bent almost double, worked his way to his patient's side. "How are you feeling, Ruth?"

She looked at him through enormous brown eyes and smiled faintly. In the light from the single lantern hanging overhead, her skin appeared almost transparent. She swallowed with some difficulty, and her words were barely audible as she said, "Not much better, I am afraid."

Noah looked with some resentment at the doctor. "Her fever is worse," he said, unable to keep the awful, constricting fear out of his voice. His eyes were wild with grief, his old face gaunt with concern.

Throckmorton looked away from Noah and smiled gently down at Ruth. "I have some opium left to ease you," he told her, opening his bag.

Her bony hand reached out suddenly and clasped Throckmorton's wrist. Through her grasp, he could feel the fire raging within her. She was like a wood-frame building on fire, with only the shell still standing.

"Will it cure me, Braden?" she asked in that ghostly whisper.

Throckmorton hesitated for a moment, then shook his head.

"Then don't give it to me. It makes my head so fuzzy. I want it clear now." She paused to get her breath. "I want it clear so I can . . . talk to Noah."

The doctor closed his bag.

"Leave us be now, Braden," she whispered. "Noah and I want to say good-bye to each other." She released his wrist. "Go! Please!"

His throat suddenly constricting, Throckmorton nodded stiffly and backed hastily out of the wagon. Glancing back one last time as he stepped down, he saw Noah cradling his wife's head in his arms.

Turning swiftly, he rushed off through the chill darkness.

Ruth died early the next day and was buried that same afternoon on a gentle rise set back from the trail. The ground was too hard and unyielding for a cross to be driven into it or for a deep-enough grave to be dug, so a stone cairn was fashioned over Ruth's blanketed body to protect it from the wolves. Over that crude memorial, Deacon Smathers spoke again of his just and terrible God and the forgiveness he knew for certain lay in wait for Ruth Whittington on the other side.

The words meant nothing to Noah. From the moment he felt the chill creep through Ruth's frail body and into his own, he lived as in a dream. He heard voices and saw people passing before him. At times he was able to reply to their questions or nod at their remarks, but this didn't fool him. For he knew he, too, had died.

But why, he wondered, did he have to remain here in this terrible place while Ruth went on ahead of him? It made no sense, no sense at all. What was he to do walking the earth without her?

A kind of resentment crept into his thinking. Why had she abandoned him in this fashion? What had he done? She had never left him in all the years they had been together. He found himself trying to recall a time when she had not been at his side. It was impossible. There couldn't have been such a time—and if there had been, it mustn't have been of any consequence. They had become like twins born of the same womb. And now separated.

Someone patted Noah gently on the back. He glanced up to see Scott Winslow peering at him with some concern.

"We're pulling out now, Noah," Winslow told him gently. "There's been more Indian signs, so we can't delay any longer."

Noah nodded carefully, then moistened his dry lips. "I will stay by Ruth for a moment longer," he told Winslow. "Would someone lead my wagon up here to me? I'll follow after shortly."

Noah saw the hesitation in Winslow's eyes.

"Please, Scott," the old man whispered, his voice almost breaking. "I must say good-bye alone." He waved his bony arm at the crowd of wagons clustered below the knoll. "Without all this commotion."

Reluctantly, Winslow nodded. "All right, Noah, but dammit, don't stay too long."

"No, Scott. I won't."

"I'll have Tim lead your wagon up here for you."

Noah watched the big man move off. A moment later, Tim drove his wagon up the gentle rise and left it on the other side of the cairn. Tim started to walk toward Noah, but thought better of it—out of consideration for his feelings, Noah was sure—and hurried back down the slope. Noah watched the wagon train, with the stagecoach in front, as it moved off, the rumble of wagon wheels on hard ground like distant thunder.

The trail curved out of sight behind a shelving ridge of pine, and it wasn't long before the last wagon vanished. Noah quickly stepped up into his wagon and drove the nervous team back down onto the trail. He propped his blanket roll end up on the seat behind the reins and placed his black, floppy-brimmed hat on top of it. Then he stepped down from the wagon, slapped the reins down hard upon the backs of his horses, and wound them swiftly around the brake lever.

The horses started up obediently, but then slowed, puzzled by Noah's odd behavior. Stepping forward, he slapped the nearest horse smartly on the rump, then reached over quickly and again flicked the reins.

"Gee-up!" he shouted angrily. "Damn your hides!"

That was enough for them. The four horses shook their massive heads in resentment at such uncalled-for treatment and started off at a brisk trot, anxious to catch up with the rest of the wagons.

Noah climbed back up to Ruth and watched the wagon disappear. Then he moved closer to the cairn and let himself down on the cold earth beside it, resting his cheek on one of the stones. He lost track of time. The sun's warmth faded and the ground grew colder.

When the first shadow fell over him, he didn't bother to look up. When a second joined the first, he shivered and clutched the rocks as the first arrow, then a second, slammed into his back.

The pain was searing. But only for an instant.

Chapter 11

It was Bill Walsh who first noticed how far behind the rest of the wagon train Noah's wagon had lagged. Worried despite Candy's insistence that the old man probably just wanted to nurse his sorrow in private, Bill shouted ahead to the next wagon that something might be wrong with Noah. His message was passed along the line, and it was Deacon Smathers who shouted the concern to Winslow. At once Winslow asked Throckmorton to stand up and look back to see if he could catch a glimpse of Noah's wagon.

"I can see Bill Walsh's wagon," Throckmorton told him as he peered back up the trail. "And that's all. Noah should be right behind him. But there's a lot of bends in the trail. His wagon might be just behind that last stand of pine."

"Keep looking," Winslow told him.

Winslow began to slow the team. He didn't want to stop—not with all those Indian signs Tim had been picking up lately. But he sure as hell wasn't going to take this wagon train much farther without making sure Noah was all right.

141

He hadn't liked the way Noah had reacted to his wife's death. It had gutted the old man, snuffed out his soul. For a few anxious moments as Winslow had driven away from Ruth's burial site, he had gotten the queer feeling that Noah might not want to rejoin the wagon train—that he might choose to stay with his wife until the cold or whatever claimed him. That had been why, after going only a short distance from the cairn, he had slowed the wagon train until he had seen Noah's wagon pulling back in line.

"Still can't see Noah's wagon," Throckmorton commented, a note of concern creeping into his voice.

"Dammit!" Winslow said, hauling back on the ribbons.

As he climbed down, Kate poked her head out of the coach window. "What is it? And don't tell me 'later' this time."

"Noah's let his wagon drop too far behind. I don't like it. I'm sending Tim back to check on it."

As he said this, he saw the sudden frown on Terry Lambert's face. She had crowded up to the coach window alongside Kate the moment Winslow came over.

"Do you think something has happened to Noah?" Kate asked.

"He was in pretty bad shape after Ruth's death. That's all I know."

Winslow moved on past the stage. Deacon Smathers had climbed down and was standing beside his wagon. Together the two of them approached Tim Curry's wagon.

Tim saw them coming and handed the reins to Thomas Grant, who had found a home of sorts with Tim. For the last few days, Grant had been a lot quieter. For all of them—certainly for Tim—that was a relief. But for just an instant as Winslow glanced at Grant, he wondered if he hadn't caught a hint of madness in Grant's furtive eyes.

Winslow hastily dismissed the thought, so concerned was he over Noah.

Tim eased himself down from the wagon. His weak leg was acting up again, it looked like.

"You think that leg is strong enough to let you do some riding?" Winslow asked, his voice reflecting his anxiety about Noah.

"Don't worry about my leg. It's fine. What do you think's holding Noah up?"

"That's what I want you to find out."

"He could be asleep," Tim said hopefully.

"I hope that's it."

"Just let me get the gray saddled," Tim said, starting for the rear of his wagon.

He unhitched the gray from its tether and swiftly threw on his saddle. Climbing up into it a moment later, he looked down at Winslow and suggested he might want to start up the wagon train, just in case.

"Grant can drive my wagon, and I can catch up easy enough. Noah's got some fine horses there."

Winslow nodded. "All right, we'll keep going. But you keep your eyes peeled. And make sure that Henry's loaded."

Tim knew perfectly well what lay behind that warning, but he only nodded casually and pulled his mount around, lifting the animal to a canter. He had seen the concern in Winslow's eyes and found it mirrored in his own heart. Without wishing to alarm anyone, Tim realized, Winslow was fearful that something bad—very bad—had happened to Noah Whittington.

Tim was at full gallop when he passed the last wagon, and Candy and Bill Walsh waved at him. Glancing back at the trail, Tim felt his heart sink. Despite the wagon train having held up, there was still no sign of Noah's wagon on the trail ahead.

The wagon train was soon out of sight. The foothills closed in on Tim as the trail, broad and leisurely, wound back up toward the peaks lifting into the sky ahead of him. It was an awesome, primal wilderness through which the wagon train had journeyed, and it filled Tim with a sense of his own impermanence—and vulnerability. Now, with each beat of his horse's hooves, his desperate apprehension for old Noah Whittington grew.

Leaning his mount around a sharp bend in the trail, he almost lost his hat as he grabbed his rifle, yanked the gray to a halt, and leaped from the still-moving horse. As he flung himself to the ground, he levered a fresh cartridge into the Henry's firing chamber and watched as Red Feather's band, in the act of riding toward him, pulled up with almost comical suddenness. They were familiar with Curry's awesome weapon by this time.

Tim saw no sign of Noah, but the braves had his wagon. He could see it beyond the Indians, where they had pulled it over to the side of the trail and littered its contents all over the ground surrounding it. The sight saddened Tim profoundly, filling him with a choking rage. He took aim at the nearest mounted brave and fired. The distance was too great, however, and seeing this, the Indian uttered a shattering war whoop and lifted his lance, shaking it at Tim.

That was when Tim noticed the cottony-haired scalp attached just below the head of the brave's lance.

With a series of triumphant cries, the braves rode back to the wagon. One of their number jumped down onto its seat. His sharp yell galvanized Noah's team and the horses bolted. The Indian turned the team and then drove the wagon back up the trail, followed closely by the rest of Red Feather's band, their fierce shouts echoing among the hills long after they had passed from Tim's sight.

Tim stood up and gazed miserably after them, the thought of Noah's fate filling him with a numbing sorrow. Almost reluctantly, he retrieved his gray and mounted up. Red Feather might allow himself to be satisfied with no more than an old man's scalp and the plunder of his single wagon, but Tim found this difficult to believe. The half-breed had already paid too dear a price to be willing to settle for so paltry a prize. Wasting no more time, Tim rode back at full gallop, overtaking the wagons with still more than a few hours of daylight left.

Winslow pulled the stage to a halt as soon as he saw the rider approach. Though Winslow was upset upon hearing the news of Noah's death, he obviously had been prepared for such news and took it well. But when Tim told the others, he saw the shattering fear and pain in their eyes. The preacher seemed unusually affected. He mumbled something about God's judgment on them all and moved off. With a sigh, Tim tied his horse to the rear of his wagon and climbed up beside Grant.

As he took the reins back from the man, Terry Lambert appeared beside the wagon.

"They said you fired at the Indians," she said. Her face was flushed and Tim guessed she had been running.

"That's right."

"But you were alone."

"I had my Henry," he told her, smiling. "It's like having ten men."

"I was worried. Very worried."

"You didn't need to be, Terry. But thank you."

"I guess I'm being foolish, aren't I."

"I don't think so."

"Yes, I am."

And then she was gone.

Terry's concern lifted Tim's spirits immensely. He recalled how good it was to be with her, and shook his head in wonder. What in hell was wrong with him? Or with her? After all, she was just one of Kate Harrow's girls.

Two days later, with no further sign of Red Feather or his renegades, Winslow found it more difficult to find men willing to stand guard. But when he insisted, as he finally had to, whatever reluctance there was immediately vanished. There was no one in the wagon train—with the possible exception of Bill Walsh—who would seriously consider contradicting Winslow—not after the way he had led them across that divide through a howling maelstrom of snow and sleet.

It was while he was checking out Throckmorton, who was on guard at the outer fringe of the pine grove in which they were camped, that the doctor pulled him close to ask a surprising question.

"What's going on with the preacher, Winslow? You got any idea?"

Winslow frowned. "I think I've been too busy shepherding this gang to notice. He's been keeping his head down some, I notice. But I suppose that's natural—after the way his handpicked wagon master turned out. Besides, the death of the Whittingtons has shaken him considerably." He looked for a long moment at the doctor. "Now just why in tarnation did you ask that question?"

"I thought you'd never ask."

"Out with it. What have you heard?"

"I have heard nothing. But I count myself as a reasonably astute student of human nature, and to these eyes something—as the Immortal Bard once said—is rotten in the state of Denmark."

"This isn't Denmark, Doctor."

"And a good thing it isn't. But still, Winslow, you should keep your eye on that man. There is trouble afoot. I can feel it."

"I hope you're wrong, Throckmorton. But right now, it's Red Feather and his band I'm worried about. So keep *your* eyes—and ears—open. We're not out of this yet. As you said yourself, Red Feather is a persistent sonofabitch."

Throckmorton winced. "Thank you for leaving me with that comforting thought. May all your nightmares be long ones."

With a brief smile, Winslow moved off.

Though he had tried not to show it, Winslow shared Throckmorton's concern. Kate had hinted at trouble the day before, but had been reluctant to say anything specific. Something, it was clear, was bothering Smathers. But Winslow had no idea what this could be. There was some talk about the deacon and Candy Walsh, but this was so far out of line that Winslow dismissed it out of hand. But there *was* something wrong. That much was certain.

Vaguely troubled, he continued on his rounds. There was no moon, and the night was dark and strangely quiet.

Inside her wagon, Candy gasped. Then, with a tiny cry of delight, she threw her arms around the deacon's neck, hugging him still closer to her. For a frightening yet delicious moment, Smathers thought she might strangle him. Sighing softly, she loosened her arms and rested her head back, looking up into his face with wide-eyed wonder.

"Oh, Deacon Smathers," she whispered. "Do you really think we should be doing this? I mean, it's almost sinful—to feel this good. Don't you think?"

"God meant us to have pleasure," Smathers replied, almost fiercely.

"I didn't mean to get you angry," Candy said, her voice hushed and repentant. "I just wondered, that's all."

"It is not something to wonder about," he told her, stroking her silken blond tresses, feeling the warmth of her naked body. "I told you, it is God's will."

147

Deacon Smathers felt an overwhelming sense of love and fulfillment—and exultant triumph. That this lovely creature should turn to him—not only as a man of God, but as a man in his own right—was a miracle to him, pure and simple. That he should be so favored was unassailable evidence that God favored him. No longer need he doubt his terrible God's infinite Grace. The ineffable sweetness of this lovely woman in his arms testified to that glorious truth.

Candy flung her arms around Smathers's neck again and drew his lips down onto hers. Clinging to him, she drank deep, her wicked tongue causing a second conflagration in his vitals. He pulled back in wonder at Candy's insatiable appetite, and for a moment considered whether or not he should chastise her. Then he kissed her again, dismissing any such thought.

"Oh, Deacon Smathers," Candy whispered, nibbling on his left earlobe. "You make me feel like a real woman."

"Call me Paul," he told her, his voice hoarse with passion. "My name is Paul."

"And you can call me Candy," she giggled. "Am I as sweet to you as candy?"

"Sweeter. Sweeter, my love," he told her, his lips moving down over the lovely, intoxicating warmth of her breasts.

A sudden, blinding light flooded over them. With a tiny cry, Candy pushed the deacon off her breasts and snatched at a sheet to cover her nakedness. Blinking up at the light, Smathers saw Bill Walsh, a kerosene lantern in his right hand, leaning into the wagon. Walsh's face was livid with fury.

"What the hell are you doing with my woman, preacher?" he demanded, his voice trembling with outrage.

"*Your* woman! How dare you! I know the truth of

148

your relationship with this poor girl. Leave this wagon, Walsh!''

"Leave this wagon?" Walsh cried. "Leave this wagon? Where in hell do you think you are, preacher? This is my wagon! And you're in here plowing my wife!''

Reaching down and grabbing the deacon by the only stitch of clothing he still had on—his woolen shirt—Bill Walsh hauled Smathers closer to him. "Damn your hide! I'm going to expose you for what you are—a lecherous, deceiving adulterer!''

"But Candy says she isn't your wife! She has been forced to accompany you west against her will!''

"I said nothing of the sort!" Candy cried. Abruptly, she buried her face in her hands and began to sob. "You just threw yourself at me!" she insisted through her sobs. "At the river that first night. And below the pass, when it was snowing. And that time in your wagon. What was I supposed to do? A man of the cloth, and all. You told me it was God's will—that we were simply pleasing God.'' She looked at him squarely then, the tears coursing down her lovely cheeks. "You promised me eternal salvation!''

Smathers was horrified. In this quiet night, Candy's terrible accusation would carry the length and breadth of the encampment. "Please, Candy! Enough! I told you nothing of the sort. You . . . misunderstood me!''

And then, to the preacher's stunned astonishment, Candy leaned her head back and began to laugh. "Like hell I did, preacher!" she cried, grinning with delight at his consternation. "Eternal grace! That's what I was sup-posed to get in your arms! You said we were pleasing God? Hell, you didn't even please *me*!''

"But . . . but Candy! What are you saying? Why are you laughing?''

The preacher's head was spinning. This incredible

scene should have been part of a nightmare; instead, it was really happening!

Then it was Bill Walsh's turn. Chuckling, the burly fellow dragged Smathers brutally from the wagon. Flinging him to the ground, Walsh reached back into the wagon and threw the deacon's britches after him.

"Go back to your wagon, preacher!" Walsh shouted for all to hear. "And don't let me catch you messin' with Candy again. Not unless you make an appointment—and pay in advance!" Then he threw his head back and laughed heartily, Candy's own shrill laughter mingling with his.

Staring up at them from the ground, the deacon realized how completely he had been used these past weeks.

"Good night, Paul!" Candy sang, dropping the wagon's rear curtain.

Laughing, Bill Walsh vanished behind the wagon, his laughter hanging in the air after him, a mockery that cut cruelly into Smathers as he frantically pulled on his trousers and fled through the blessed darkness to his own wagon.

From Terry Lambert's tent across the clearing, she and Tim Curry had seen and heard everything. Watching through a slit in the canvas, they saw the deacon slink away like a thief in the night.

Terry turned away from the slit and looked into Tim's eyes. "How awful," she said. "What a terrible thing to do to a man. She was just leading him on all this time."

Tim nodded glumly. "I suppose the preacher deserved it, but you're right. It was a terribly cruel thing to do."

Terry shuddered in distaste and looked away from Tim's honest, concerned face.

"Terry," Tim asked gently, "you wouldn't do such a thing to me, would you?"

"What a thing to ask," she said, scolding him. "Of course not! What kind of a person do you think I am?"

"I'm sorry. That was a stupid question, I suppose. But sometimes, a guy can get pretty confused when it comes to a woman."

She caught the note in his voice and became suddenly alarmed. They were veering dangerously close to a topic Terry had been careful to keep away from at all times. "Just relax," she soothed. "You know how it is with us, don't you? We're just . . . comforting each other."

"Oh, sure," Tim replied hastily, "I didn't mean it was anything more than that."

Terry rested her forehead against Tim's bare shoulder so he wouldn't be able to see the disappointment in her face or the tears that now crowded into the corners of her eyes. She realized, to her own dismay, that she had been hoping against hope that Tim would have protested that it was more than comfort they were offering each other now. Much more.

But what did she expect? She was a whore. And a man like Tim Curry wouldn't fall in love with a whore.

Reaching his wagon, Deacon Smathers crawled onto his cot. The sound of Candy's laughter was still ringing so shrilly in his ears that he was certain he would go mad.

He saw now with terrible clarity that from the very beginning Candy and Bill Walsh had been preparing for this shameful night. To them, he had been a source of amusement—something with which to while away the dreary hours of this interminable trek west.

His soul writhing in torment as the full horror struck him, Smathers recalled every shameful act of lust, every endearment he had spoken to Candy. Why, once he had even wept openly in her arms! A whore! She was a whore! Yet in her arms he had confided his most secret, his most private thoughts. He had opened his soul to her—assuming all the while that they would be married at the end of their journey. In the name of God's everlasting glory, he had taken her. He had consorted with one of Satan's angels and hadn't realized, until it was too late, the awful extent of his befoulment!

But that wasn't the worst of it.

He knew now that he didn't have—that he had never had—his God's Grace. The deaths of three of his flock, and now this great shame, were proof of this dark truth. Now the numbing truth was clear for all to see. He was doomed. With mounting horror, he saw in the darkness of his lonely wagon an image of himself that shriveled his soul. As he witnessed this terrible vision, he stuck the knuckles of his right hand into his mouth to prevent his scream from ripping through the encampment.

God's great hand had been holding him over the abyss. Now, as Smathers watched, the great hand opened, releasing the twisted, screaming soul of Deacon Smathers, casting it into the fiery pit. Down, down, into the maw of Hell his Immortal Soul plunged. And as it did, Smathers felt himself being swallowed up in the terrible, incinerating heat of that eternal hellfire. . . .

At last he could contain his terror no longer. He screamed. And every living soul in the encampment heard his scream—and understood.

The journey continued in silence the next day, and that night the wagon train made camp in a meadow beside a small mountain lake. There was little joviality as the settlers tended to their fires and prepared themselves for the night's rest. Only with great care did anyone converse with the deacon, and no one allowed himself to speak directly to Candy and Bill Walsh. For by this time there wasn't a single person in the wagon train—with the possible exception of Thomas Grant—who didn't know what those two had done to Deacon Smathers.

After checking on the guards, Winslow stopped back at the stagecoach. The ground behind it was solid with tents, and in one of them, Melody and Collette could be heard laughing. After the melancholy business of the previous night, it was a welcome sound. They were almost out of the mountains now, and Red Feather's threat seemed to have vanished. The girls' laughter seemed to transform that hope into reality.

Kate stepped out of her tent to stand in the chill darkness beside Scott. "How's the preacher doing?" she asked softly.

"He's in his wagon. He didn't bother to make a fire. I doubt if he had supper."

Kate shook her head and sighed. "I wasn't crazy about Smathers," she said, "but I have no use at all for folks who'd do something as pointlessly cruel as what was done to that poor fool."

Winslow said nothing. He understood Kate's outrage and felt it himself. But what worried him now was whether the deacon would be able to survive such a crushing blow to his self-esteem. He had been revealed as an adulterer to everyone in the wagon train. Even worse, he had been revealed to himself as being thoroughly human.

"Are you still worried about Red Feather?" Kate asked, breaking into Winslow's thoughts.

"Yes. As long as we're still in the mountains."

"But soon we'll be in the valley."

"Yes. Soon."

She took a deep breath and then looked quizzically up at Winslow. "Will you continue to drive the stagecoach all the way to Seattle?"

"Yes. That was the deal, I believe."

She nodded, seemingly relieved. He was mildly

amused. Had she been afraid he would run off and leave her to drive the stage herself?

"What are your plans, Kate—I mean after you reach Seattle?"

"Do you really want to know?"

Winslow smiled, shrugging. "I just wanted to know if you were going to continue with your . . . profession."

"What else is there for me?"

He could feel the infinite weariness in Kate's reply, and out of deference for her feelings, he didn't press the matter any further. But Kate seemed willing enough to discuss it.

"I had thought of getting out, you know," she said. "There's a gentleman in Seattle who says he'd be pleased to have my company on a more or less permanent basis—without the benefit of matrimony, of course."

"Oh?"

"I admit, it was a tempting offer."

"Was?"

She nodded and looked up at him, her gaze bold. At once Winslow knew why she had decided against accepting her gentleman friend's offer. It was meeting Winslow that had changed her mind. It flattered him to know this—but it alarmed him as well, and he felt himself involuntarily pulling back. How could he expect any kind of sensible involvement with a madam? She was a handsome woman, for sure. But where Winslow hailed from, handsome is as handsome does.

It saddened him to see how quickly Kate sensed his pulling back. But she had plenty of sand, he noted, and continued to smile up at him without the slightest malice.

"What are *your* plans, Scott?" she asked, tipping her head slightly. "I doubt if visiting the town of Seattle was one of your life's ambitions."

"You're right. When you pay me off, I'll move on, I guess."

"Move on? To where?"

"That's a good question. I don't know."

"There's no . . . person, no particular place?"

"No place—nobody," Scott replied bluntly.

"I see. Do you mind, Scott, if I ask what you were doing in Baker?"

"Gambling."

"I got the impression it was more than that."

"I was waiting. But I wasn't too sure myself what it was I was waiting for. Three years ago, I started looking for someone, and I guess I was still looking for him."

"Looking for someone? Who, or shouldn't I ask?"

Scott regarded Kate for a moment, then decided it wouldn't do any harm to tell her about Matt Cord. It might even help her understand a few things. When he had finished, she shook her head in wonderment.

"How odd," she said. "How very odd, the way things turn out. Makes you wonder, doesn't it."

"Yes, Kate. It does."

"So now you have no one to search for—no reason for keeping your weapon ready." She smiled ironically. "I suppose you feel rootless now, without purpose. Is that it, Scott?"

It was alarming how clearly she saw his dilemma. Her words weren't meant as a rebuke, but he felt rebuked, nevertheless. As she put it so simply, he was rootless, a man without a purpose.

He nodded. "I suppose that says it all, Kate."

"Then you suppose wrong. Don't you see, Scott? You weren't able to kill Matt Cord, though you could have, whenever you wished. Any excuse would have sufficed. You could have goaded him, forced him to draw. But you didn't."

"The sonofabitch had saved my life."

"That wasn't why you didn't go for him, Scott. You didn't because you saw clearer than that. Don't you understand? You had found a different, better goal—one that made you proud and worth something in your own eyes."

He looked at her, his eyes narrowing. What, he wondered, did this woman know about him that he didn't know about himself? "I don't see it, Kate. What are you driving at?"

"This wagon train, Scott. And me and the girls. We needed you, and you knew that. From the first, you realized our problem. And then, when we finally crossed that river, you assumed responsibility for all of us. And from then on, Scott, you were no longer a man without a purpose."

"If that's true, what now? We'll reach our destination soon enough, and I'll have no more wagon train to lead."

"There are other responsibilities you can shoulder, Scott—just as important. It's up to you to find them. And you will, if you'll stop telling yourself that you're rootless. You aren't—not unless you want to be."

What Kate was telling him was something he had felt dimly, but had been unable to get a clear handle on—until now, until Kate spoke. He looked at her with new awareness and appreciation.

"Thanks, Kate," he said, "Maybe I'll give that some thought."

Smiling almost awkwardly, Winslow touched the brim of his hat and moved on. He had to check on Tim Curry. The man had been on guard for close to four hours, and it was about time Winslow relieved him.

Chapter 12

As Winslow cut through a thin stand of pine on his way to Tim Curry's guard post, a tall figure materialized before him in the darkness. The full moon was bright enough for Winslow to recognize the man easily.

Red Feather was proving once again just how persistent he was.

As Winslow reached for his Colt, Red Feather raised his hand, palm out. "I want Grant," he said. "Give me Grant and I will leave you and the rest of the wagon train in peace."

"No. I couldn't do that, Red Feather. Why do you want him?"

"Grant warned you. He fooled us—fooled all of us. We thought he was crazy, but he wasn't. Give him to us, and we will find out for sure."

"The way you found out about Matt Cord?"

"He was a man with no worth. Why do you care what happened to him?"

Winslow shrugged. He found it difficult to argue with that. Nevertheless, there was no way Red Feather could convince him to hand over Grant.

"I won't let you take him, Red Feather. Go back to the mountains. Let us finish our journey in peace."

"If you will not give us Grant, then we will take you, wagon master."

"Now, what good would that do you?"

He smiled. "Without you, this wagon train will fall like ripe berries into our hands. And then we shall see about this valley we approach. I have already scouted it. It is time for harvest, and that is what we shall do. There is much to plunder there."

"Is that all you think of, Red Feather? Plundering and killing?"

"Yes. It is all I think of when I think of the white man."

"There is white blood in you, I have heard."

The Indian appeared to seethe. "With the death of each white face, I purge a drop of that defilement from my soul. Do you understand such hate, wagon master?"

"It is too bad you were never taught of love, as well as hate."

"Hate is strong. Love is weak. But enough of this. We will take you with us. It will be interesting to see what lies in your soul. Perhaps you will die with courage. I hope so. Now come."

Winslow could have cried out for help, but he saw no reason to endanger the others. Despite Winslow's precautions, Red Feather's braves evidently had been able to infiltrate the encampment without detection. His only chance was to take Red Feather himself. It was a long shot, but he had drawn to an inside straight before and won.

Winslow ducked back and drew his Colt. Before he could get off a shot, however, two of Red Feather's braves sprang from the trees. One gripped his shoulders from behind. The other knocked the Colt from his hand and grabbed his arm. Winslow twisted forward and flung one of the braves ahead of him. Then, spinning around, he managed to break loose of the second brave.

But before he could run, Red Feather's rifle butt slammed into the back of his skull. He felt himself sprawling forward into darkness—and was unconscious before he hit the ground.

Tim Curry had heard voices coming from the pines. Moving stealthily, he slipped through the moon-washed darkness and was just in time to see at least three braves, with Red Feather in the lead, dragging someone through the trees away from the camp. From the heft of the fellow they were dragging, Tim had no doubt whom they had captured: Scott Winslow.

Even as Tim watched, he saw two other Indians slipping out of the woods to join Red Feather. There were too many for Tim, and if he fired now in this poor light, he just might hit Winslow. Turning, he raced back to the encampment, coming first upon Phil Turner in front of his wagon.

"Get your rifle!" Tim told him, his voice lowered to a hoarse whisper. "Red Feather's got Scott!"

Grant heard Tim and came running, his eyes wild. "Red Feather!" he cried.

"Get back to the wagon," Tim told the man. "I want you to stay here in the encampment and keep a lookout."

Reluctantly, Grant nodded and backed hastily toward Tim's wagon.

Beechwood appeared from the other side of the encampment. He had heard Grant's sudden outcry and had begun to run toward Tim the moment he caught sight of Phil climbing down out of his wagon with his rifle in his hand.

"What's up?" Beechwood demanded as he came up beside Tim.

Tim told the man what he had seen. Then, satisfied they could wait no longer, he led Phil and Joshua in a swift trot back through the pines. The moon was bright enough for them to follow the Indians' tracks as they hurried through the woodland, and it wasn't long before they came upon a bright clearing and saw the Indians heading toward their horses, which were tethered on the far side.

Pulling up, Tim crouched low and turned to the others. "You two stay here," he told them. "I've got the fire-power with this Henry to turn those savages. I'll circle around and open up on them, driving them back into your fire. But don't shoot unless you have a clear target—otherwise you might hit Scott."

"You didn't have to tell me that," growled Beechwood.

Tim didn't take offense and with a quick nod, glided swiftly off into the pines.

Phil Turner moistened his lips and waited. Beside him, Beechwood appeared just as nervous.

"Ready?" Beechwood asked softly. "All primed?"

Phil nodded, not daring to speak. He could see clear to the other side of the moonlit meadow, where the braves had just reached their mounts. A few were already swinging into their saddles. One of them—Red Feather, from the look of him—reached down and roughly pulled the unconscious prisoner over the neck of his pony.

Red Feather held up while the rest of his war party mounted up. Phil counted nine Indians in all. Abruptly, from the cover of brush on the far side of the war party, Tim Curry opened up. Two Indians were cut down with astonishing rapidity. Another Indian, already mounted, tried to rush Tim and was shot off his horse.

160

Phil heard Red Feather's shout of warning then and saw the chieftain spin his horse around and charge back across the clearing, directly toward Phil and Joshua.

"Remember what Tim said," Joshua whispered. "Make sure you have a clear target. And watch out for Winslow."

Phil picked out an Indian riding alongside Red Feather, waited calmly until the brave was clearly in his sight, then squeezed the trigger. The rifle bucked and the Indian slumped, then rolled off his mount. Red Feather turned his horse directly toward Phil then, just as Joshua cut down a second brave. With Red Feather bearing down on him, Phil frantically reloaded, but realized at the last moment that he didn't have enough time.

Grasping his rifle by the barrel, he quickly stepped out into the clearing and swung, catching Red Feather chest high. He heard a sharp grunt as the half-breed was knocked back off his horse. The pony, with the still-unconscious Winslow on its back, vanished into the woods behind Phil, following what remained of Red Feather's band.

Groggy from the blow and still on his hands and knees, Red Feather shook his head to clear it. Seeing his chance, Phil pulled out his long hunting knife and rushed him. Red Feather was still armed, however. Rolling swiftly away as Phil attacked, he leaped to his feet and discharged his rifle. The round caught Phil in the side, just under his rib cage, knocking him back. His head spinning from the shock of the blow, he sagged to one knee. Red Feather unsheathed his own knife and slashed at Phil. Desperately, the young man managed to parry the Indian's first thrust with his own hunting knife, but the wound had so weakened him that he sagged helplessly to the ground.

In that instant Phil saw Joshua lying on the ground unconscious—or dead—beside what appeared to be a dead Indian. The three braves still on their mounts had pulled up in the woods as soon as Red Feather went down, and could be heard now riding back through the timber to aid their leader.

It was all over, Phil realized, as he saw Red Feather looming over him, his long buffalo knife gleaming in the moonlight, his savage face distorted with hate. Though Phil knew he should try to roll away, all he could do was wait for the knife stroke to descend.

A rifle shot cracked from the woods just behind Phil, and Red Feather spun to the ground, his knife flying. A second later, Tim Curry raced from the far side of the clearing and got off a shot that nicked one of the Indians riding back through the woods. The wounded savage managed to stay on his horse and turn it, and with him in the lead, the three mounted braves galloped back into the timber and out of sight.

As Tim rushed up, Phil turned his head in time to see Kate Harrow step from cover, a long, gleaming rifle in her hand. It was she who had shot Red Feather. And from behind her stumbled Scott Winslow, rubbing his throbbing head.

Around noon the next day, his head still thundering from the blow he had received the night before, Scott Winslow listened intently to what Dr. Throckmorton was telling him. Both Phil Turner and Red Feather had bullets lodged in their bodies that had to be removed if they were to recover. One slug had remained in Phil's right side, just under his rib cage. The other slug—the one fired by Kate Harrow—had burrowed into Red Feather's neck, close to the jugular. The operations to remove the slugs would be comparatively simple, Throckmorton assured Winslow. The only problem was that they only had whiskey for an anesthetic.

"What do you want me to do?" Winslow asked.

"I want you to hold them down," Throckmorton replied.

Winslow didn't much like the idea, but he nodded and said, "Lead the way."

As Winslow hurried across the campsite alongside Throckmorton, he found himself marveling at how lucky he had been to have escaped with just a sore head. And Joshua Beechwood had been lucky, too. He was suffering what the doctor diagnosed as a severe concussion, and at the moment he was resting in his wagon under the care of his frantic wife. The Indian he had shot from his horse had landed on him with almost killing force, knocking him senseless to the ground.

The doctor had fashioned a makeshift hospital in among the pines. With cots he had taken from the wagons, he had been able to bed the wounded men under the protection of some extra canvas. Mary Turner was beside her husband's cot, stroking Phil's fair hair, her eyes devouring his with love and concern.

Red Feather had both hands bound in front of him, and several strands of rope were wound tightly around his torso, effectively securing him to the cot. Earlier, though barely conscious at the time, he had tried to strangle Terry Lambert. She had been bent over him, attempting to stanch the blood flowing from his neck wound.

Kate and her girls had been pressed into service as Throckmorton's assistants. It was Kate who held the whiskey bottle. Beside her stood Terry Lambert with the doctor's tray of instruments. Melody and Collette were holding buckets of steaming hot compresses at the ready, as well as freshly laundered bandages.

"All right, Kate," Throckmorton said.

"Excuse me, Mary," said Kate, as she stepped closer to Phil.

Unscrewing the cap, Kate held the bottle out to Phil. Grinning feebly, he opened his mouth to accept the drink. In careful but generous doses, Kate administered the potion. Soon enough, Phil's eyes grew glassy, and with a silly grin on his face, he pushed the bottle away.

At once Throckmorton went to work. With astonishing speed, he probed under Phil's breast for the errant bullet. Phil began to struggle. Winslow bent over and, placing both hands on the lad's shoulders, leaned forward heavily to restrain him.

"Got it!" muttered the doctor, holding up the tweezers. Then he tossed the bullet aside and beckoned Melody closer for the hot compresses she was holding. Again the doctor worked rapidly as he applied the compresses to the wound and wrapped a bandage tightly around Phil's torso, effectively sealing the wound.

Phil took a deep breath and glanced over at Kate. "How about another swig from the bottle?" he asked weakly.

With a smile, Kate obliged.

"Next," said the doctor, turning his attention to Red Feather.

As Kate carefully approached the Indian with her bottle of whiskey, Red Feather shook his head violently. She made a tentative attempt to give the Indian the anesthetic, then pulled back, glancing with some confusion at Scott Winslow.

Remembering Matt Cord's ribboned body, Winslow said, "Never mind, Kate. I'll hold the sonofabitch. He doesn't need anything."

Kate stepped back, and Winslow took a place beside Red Feather and waited for the doctor to go to work. Again, Throckmorton's speed was remarkable as he probed the wound in the Indian's neck just above his breastbone. It took a little longer than it had with Phil, but the Indian didn't utter a sound or make any attempt to pull away. Instead, he kept his cold blue eyes focused on Winslow.

At last, with a deep sigh, Throckmorton pulled out the round. He didn't bother to flaunt it, but merely flung it aside and proceeded to pack the wound and then bandage it. He was as swift as before, but for a moment Winslow wondered if he wasn't intent on strangling the half-breed, so tightly did he wrap the bandage around Red Feather's neck.

With a sudden, malicious grin, Throckmorton turned to Winslow. "That should hold the bastard, don't you think?"

"It should at that," Winslow agreed.

Throckmorton turned to Kate. "Now let *me* have some of that medicine, Kate. I am sorely in need."

"Be my guest," she said, handing him the bottle.

Mary looked down at her inebriated husband and smiled warmly. His large ears suddenly seemed larger as he made a face at her and rolled his eyes. In that instant she realized he still was a little boy—a little boy she loved very much. But he was also a man. He had been proving that almost every day since the trouble with the Indians began. And now, when she thought of her petulant disappointment over his troubles with the cows and the wagon, she was ashamed.

Impulsively, she kissed him full on the lips.

"Hey, what's that for?" he asked, grinning blearily up at her.

"I just felt like it," she said.

"That's not fair," he protested. "In my condition, how am I expected to return the compliment?"

She hugged him. "I'm not worried about that," she told him impishly. "You'll do so soon enough, I'm sure."

Looking up at his pretty wife with a vision still unsteady from all that alcohol, he smiled foolishly and stroked her fair hair. Yes, he would. He would soon enough return her love in full measure.

And soon enough wouldn't be too soon for him.

Amanda shook her head once more as she wrung the compress out the back of their wagon.

"You could have been killed," she told Joshua, replacing the compress with a fresh one. For good reason, Joshua was still complaining from a mild headache and a few aches and pains, liberally distributed around his long frame.

"Well, I wasn't," Joshua pointed out. "But being crushed senseless by a dead Indian is close enough. I should have known enough to get out of the way when I shot him. Not very romantic, that. I don't suppose it will ever be recorded in one of Beadle's Dime Novel adventures. I feel kind of silly, as a matter of fact."

"Now don't you say that," she said softly. Her eyes suddenly filled with love for this tough man who was really so gentle underneath.

"The worst part was his smell," Joshua went on. "I never knew an aborigine could smell like that." He was thoughtful for a moment. "Of course, I was never that close to one before."

"Shush," she said, resting her cheek against his. Her hand stole around his shoulder, and she found herself hugging him close, very close.

"Now woman," Joshua said softly, "there ain't no need for you to get all exercised."

"Yes, there is," she said softly. "And I think now is

the time.'' She took the wet compress off his forehead and laid it to one side.

Joshua chuckled, a warm, deep-throated sound that sent shivers through her. ''Guess maybe you're right at that, woman. Maybe now *is* the time.''

He kissed her on the cheek, gently. She moved her head so that their lips met as he quickly drew her onto the bed beside him. Thrusting herself eagerly against him, she seemed unwilling for the kiss to end.

Feeling her life-giving warmth flow through him, Joshua realized once again how good it was to be alive. And how grateful he was that he and Amanda had come on this long trek. For no matter what lay ahead of them now, they had found in each other what Joshua had long known was there all the time.

Satisfied that the remnants of Red Feather's renegades had retreated back into the mountains to lick their wounds, Winslow gave the order to pack up and move out. They had at least five hours of daylight left, and during that stretch, they just might make it into the valley.

Thomas Grant hurried away from the wagons, carrying a wooden bucket toward the stream. Tim had asked him to fill it before they pulled out. But once out of sight of the wagons, Grant dropped the bucket. Mumbling imprecations under his breath and with his eyes lit as if on fire, he headed back toward the makeshift hospital where Red Feather and Phil Turner were still resting. He didn't approach directly, but crept through the pines.

He held up when he heard voices, and peered through the trees. Dr. Throckmorton and Mary Turner were helping Phil back to his wagon. As soon as they were out of sight, Grant pushed through the brush and came out under the canvas, stopping beside Red Feather's cot.

The Indian, still bound and fully awake, was able to

turn his head just enough to see Grant standing over him. Grant smiled down at Red Feather, madness gleaming in his eyes, spittle drooling from one corner of his mouth. Out of his belt he drew a long butcher knife. He didn't hesitate as he raised it over his head and plunged it down into the Indian's heart. Three more times he plunged his knife into Red Feather's bloody chest. Then, with a swift flourish, he added the coup de grace, grabbing the warrior's long hair as he lifted the knife blade to his scalp.

Panting from the exertion, Thomas Grant turned and raced back through the pines.

Winslow winced, so piercing was the scream. It was Melody Tinsdale, and her scream was coming from the direction of Dr. Throckmorton's hospital tent. Dropping the harness, Winslow drew his Colt and ran full tilt for the hospital.

Scott Winslow wasn't the first to arrive—Throckmorton and Kate were there already. Kate was leading Melody away as Winslow approached.

"It's Red Feather," Throckmorton told him. "He's dead. Very dead. Someone stabbed him repeatedly in the chest—then scalped him."

By that time most of the settlers were clustered around, and Winslow spun to face them. "Where's Grant?" he demanded. "Has anyone seen Grant?"

As soon as Winslow asked the question, they knew why. Tim Curry turned and bolted back through the settlers, heading for his wagon. The rest steamed after him.

Thomas Grant was cowering under Tim's wagon, a blood-slick knife stuck in his belt, Red Feather's scalp held against his breast. He was gibbering hysterically as they approached. Abruptly, brandishing his knife, he rushed from under the wagon. Astonished, the settlers fell back away from him. Grant pulled up, laughing.

Kate stepped toward him and reached out her hand. "Give me the knife, Thomas," she said. "You don't need it anymore. Red Feather's dead."

But Grant was beyond reason. With an inarticulate cry, he lunged toward Kate.

A shot rang out, and Grant spun from the force of the bullet. Another shot followed, this second bullet slamming into Grant's skull as he hit the ground.

Astonished, Winslow spun to see Deacon Smathers slowly lowering his revolver. And what Winslow saw in the man's eyes frightened him almost as much as what he had seen a moment before in the eyes of Thomas Grant—just before the deacon killed him.

Chapter 13

Two days later, with the Blue Mountains at his back, Scott Winslow halted the stage and climbed down.

The wagon train was at a crossroads in the trail, just outside Pendleton in the Umatilla Valley. For Kate and her girls—and for Candy and Bill Walsh as well—the journey would take them north to Fort Walla Walla in Washington Territory, and from there on to Seattle. The deacon and the rest of the settlers had planned to take the trail branching to the west, which led to the Willamette Valley. After discussing the matter with some recent settlers in Pendleton, however, all of the members of the wagon train had decided to remain in the Umatilla Valley. The Willamette, they were told, was already getting too crowded. Deacon Smathers, who for so long had called the Willamette his "promised valley," had been strangely silent on the subject.

Kate and the girls stepped out of the coach as Winslow and the doctor walked over to say good-bye to the settlers. For reasons obvious to everyone, Candy and Bill Walsh kept discreetly out of sight in their wagon alongside the stage, which they would be following to Seattle.

Approaching Smathers, Winslow stuck out his hand. The deacon—more gaunt and harried-looking than ever—peered almost furtively at Winslow and attempted a smile. As enthusiastically as he could, Winslow shook the cleric's hand, but found it limp and cold. This trek had changed all of them—but for the deacon the change had been devastating.

Completely recovered from his concussion, Joshua Beechwood stood close by Amanda, his arm around her waist. He shook Winslow's hand heartily. "Next time you come by here, you look us up in Pendleton," he told Winslow. "Look for an apple orchard. A big one."

"I will," promised Winslow.

"Good luck, Scott," Tim Curry said as he stepped forward and shook his friend's hand. Winslow could see that Tim was anxiously looking for someone else—but she was back at the waiting stagecoach.

"Why don't you say good-bye to Kate and the girls?" Winslow said with a wink.

Grinning suddenly, Tim replied, "Why, I guess I might do just that."

As Tim hurried past Winslow, Mary and Phil Turner stepped forward to say good-bye.

"How's the wound?" Winslow asked.

"I can hardly feel it." He squeezed his wife suddenly. "Unless I get too active."

Mary flushed, but not with embarrassment. Then she jabbed Phil in the ribs—gently.

Tim Curry saw Terry standing beside Kate. As he approached, Kate moved discreetly away to give them some privacy. Coming to a halt before Terry, Tim swallowed nervously and wished his mouth had not gone so dry.

"I guess this is good-bye," he managed lamely.

171

"Yes," Terry replied, her smile surprisingly bright. "I guess it is."

That seemed to exhaust their store of easy conversation. Desperate, unable to comprehend the constriction that was growing in his chest, Tim cleared his throat and muttered something about how long a trip Terry still had before her.

"Yes," Terry said, as brightly as before. "It should take us another few weeks, at least. You're lucky. Do you know where you'll be settling?"

"No, I don't. I think I'll look around for a while before deciding. I think that's wise, don't you?"

"Oh, yes, I certainly do."

He looked at her with sudden intensity. "Dammit, Terry. How come we're so formal all of a sudden?"

"Why, Tim, I don't know what you mean."

"Yes, you do."

For a long moment she looked at him. "Is there something you want to say to me, Tim?"

"Well . . . isn't there something we *should* say? I mean this is good-bye, isn't it?"

"It is, if that's what you want."

"Dammit, Terry. Isn't that what you want, too?"

"Of course," Terry replied lightly. "I am most anxious to reach Seattle. Kate says it's a real boomtown, and the countryside is lovely."

Numbly, Tim nodded. He caught the desperation now in Terry's brittle cheeriness—and something else, as well. But what that might be—in her heart as well as his own—he was suddenly too frightened to face.

"Well, then," he managed, reaching out his hand. "I guess this is good-bye."

She took his hand. Her grip was firm. "Good-bye, Tim. And good luck."

She turned and stepped up into the stagecoach. He

watched her through the window until she leaned back in the seat and vanished from his sight.

Feeling a sudden and overwhelming desolation, he turned and walked back to his wagon.

Winslow was aware that precious time was passing. When he saw that Dr. Throckmorton was about finished with his flowery farewell to Phil Turner, he walked up beside him, smiling.

"Guess it's time for us to get moving, Doctor," he said. "The journey's almost over for these settlers, but we've got a few more miles to go yet."

"Right you are, my good man," replied Throckmorton. "Right you are."

Winslow stepped back and tipped the brim of his hat to the settlers, genuinely sorry to be leaving them. Though no one would openly say so, everyone realized this probably was the last time the two groups would see each other.

As the stagecoach rocked into motion, Kate Harrow leaned out and waved a last farewell to the settlers. Settling back in her seat, she glanced across at Terry Lambert and saw the tears coursing down her face, while Melody and Collette did their best not to notice. Kate kept her silence, and the stage rolled on for some distance before Kate allowed herself to reach out to Terry.

As soon as Kate's hand closed over Terry's, the young woman threw herself across the middle bench and into Kate's arms, where she exploded into shuddering, racking sobs. Kate stroked her head and spoke to her softly, doing her best to soothe Terry. But she knew there was nothing she could say that would help.

At last Terry calmed down. Looking around at the others, she blew her nose on a lace handkerchief Kate gave her and attempted a smile.

173

"I'm sorry," she managed. "I guess I'm acting a little silly."

They smiled faintly at Terry, trying to reassure her that it was all right, that they understood. Then they returned to their own thoughts. The other girls knew why Terry had broken down, and they knew there was nothing silly about it at all. They also knew the lesson it taught them: It was not a very good idea for a prostitute to fall in love with an honest man.

"I was such a fool, Kate," Terry said softly, leaning her head on Kate's shoulder. "I should have known better. You warned us."

Kate said nothing. Again, there was nothing to say.

"Forgive me," Terry whispered. "I've been so mean lately. Insufferable. I thought I knew it all. And now look at me, weeping over a man—a mere boy."

"You could have done worse. Seems to me he handled himself pretty well."

"Yes. He was wounded terribly at Shiloh. His leg is all thin and weak. But he won't let it hold him back—I know he won't." She looked suddenly into Kate's face. "Oh, Kate, why didn't you stop me? You knew that Tim and I were . . . together."

"There are some things a bystander should never get mixed up in, Terry. And a love affair is one of them."

"A love affair?"

"That's right."

Terry considered that for a long while, then shook her head in perplexity and wonder. "I didn't know love could hurt like this."

"Now you know."

"And you. I've seen you with Scott. Is it the same for you?"

Kate found herself holding Terry a little too tightly. She looked quickly out the window and nodded.

Yes. It was the same with her.

Seattle was a disappointment to Winslow. The stage had left Candy and Bill Walsh at a livery on Commercial Street. Then, following Kate's directions, Scott had driven down some muddy lanes that passed as streets, and then up one of the numerous hills along the bay. As Winslow finally pulled up in front of the raw, newly constructed frame house overlooking the sound, he realized that the girls peering out through the windows of the stage must be just as unimpressed as he. If the journey since Pendleton had been a dull anticlimax, Seattle sure as hell put the cap on it!

As heartily as he could, Winslow called down, "Here we are!"

"Goody, goody," Melody said with mock enthusiasm as she followed Kate and the others from the stagecoach.

Kate opened the front door of the house with a huge, brass skeleton key, and Throckmorton and Winslow spent most of the next two hours hauling in the trunks and heavy packing cases of books, after which Kate put them to work moving furniture. The place was damp and the furnishings were sparse. It was a chill, unexciting end to a long odyssey. But at least, as Kate told the girls, they were home now and would soon be sleeping indoors between clean sheets.

When Kate could find no more work for Winslow to do, she paid him for his services as a driver and walked with him out to the stage. The girls were watching from the downstairs living room window. When Winslow caught sight of them, he smiled and bowed slightly, then waved at Dr. Throckmorton standing in the doorway.

Kate made certain that Winslow knew the details concerning her rented stage. She had already made arrangements with the owner of the stage line operating from the

175

livery on Commercial Street, and he had agreed to hold the stage until it could be driven to a branch of the Overland Mail & Express in Portland.

That business completed, Kate seemed unwilling to say good-bye. Winslow felt the same reluctance.

"You're heading south, Braden tells me," Kate finally said.

Winslow nodded. "To San Francisco. I'll book passage on a schooner tonight or tomorrow morning."

"There's nothing that could hold you here?"

He looked for a long moment at the handsome woman beside him. "I wouldn't say that. Seattle is booming—there's no question of that. And the country around is quite beautiful—at least that part of it that isn't raw lumber and mud."

"This is a big house, Scott," she said softly. "There's plenty of room in it—for a man like you."

"It's a house, Kate—not a home."

Kate frowned. "I guess I asked for that."

"Yes, you did. That gentleman you mentioned earlier—are you still so sure you're no longer interested in him?"

"Ditwhiler?"

"If that's his name. The lumber magnate."

"I'm still sure, Scott." She smiled wanly. "But then, time and experience have a way of teaching us things. Perhaps I shouldn't be so quick to say no to a chance for some permanence."

"If permanence is what you want, Kate, check out the local cemetery. You'll find real permanence there."

He tipped his hat to Kate, then climbed up into the stagecoach box. Just a gentle flip of the ribbons sent the impatient steeds on their way. With a single wave, he vanished down the hill.

For a long while Kate stood there, looking after him. Then she turned and walked back into her house. Her step

176

was firm, and she was already planning renovations. But, even so, there were unashamed tears rolling down her cheeks.

Two hours later, his business with the livery completed and his passage already booked on a lumber schooner, Winslow was walking along Skid Road when he was accosted by Candy and Bill Walsh. They were standing outside a saloon called the Illahee, a name Winslow took no pleasure at all in pronouncing. Candy and Bill seemed genuinely relieved to see Winslow and most anxious that he join them. This was a tough town, obviously, and the only real security was in numbers—and in as many tall friends as you could muster.

"Let's go in here for a drink, Scott," Bill suggested eagerly. "Candy and I have been having some difficulty finding a place to spend an evening in this town."

"We're thinking of moving on to Olympia," Candy added.

"As soon as possible," Walsh seconded, as he pushed through the batwings with Candy and Winslow.

They found a table against a wall. The long, oblong building was fashioned of weather-beaten boards. It contained a large dance floor, flanked by a long bar. At the edge of the dance floor was a long hallway that led to the cribs of the house girls. The Indian girls providing the entertainment looked reasonably well scrubbed, and their hair was combed and cut. But aside from that, there was little else to recommend them—except that here in Seattle, as one disgruntled sailor had already complained to Winslow, there was only one female for every ten males.

Walsh ordered three beers, then turned and leered at Winslow. "A wild town, this. Looks like Kate Harrow knew what she was doing, all right. What a place for a cathouse!"

Winslow kept his expression calm and managed a civil nod. But it wasn't easy.

Their drinks arrived, and Walsh paid the Indian girl. As she turned to leave their table, he reached over and pinched her. She uttered a tiny squeal and hurried from the table. He and Candy turned to Winslow, laughing heartily at the Indian girl's reaction.

"I'm glad to see you weren't taken in by Kate," Candy told Scott. "I thought her airs were ludicrous. Who does she think she is, anyway? But I knew from the start a man like you wouldn't be taken in by such trash, no matter how gaudy the package."

Winslow sipped his beer and looked around. It took every ounce of willpower he possessed to ignore that crack, and he was looking for a way to break off this reunion fast—before he punched one of them.

What he saw, to his amazement, was Tim Curry.

"Hey, Tim!" Winslow called in sudden relief. "Over here!"

Almost knocking over a table in his haste, Tim made a beeline for Winslow and slumped into a chair at their table. "I need a drink," he said.

Winslow waved the girl over and ordered a beer. When it came, Tim downed the stein in three or four gulps, then slammed the empty glass down on the table and looked hard at Winslow.

"Have you seen Deacon Smathers?" he asked.

"The preacher? Of course not. He's back in Oregon with the settlers, isn't he?"

"No, he isn't. He lit out on horseback a few days after you left. He has snapped, Scott. He was talking crazy, raving. We tried to stop him, but he rode off like a madman. I was worried—thought it best to come after him. But I lost him this side of Fort Walla Walla."

Winslow's eyes narrowed. "Where was he heading?"

"I'm pretty sure he was on his way here."

"What the hell does he want in this place?" Bill Walsh asked.

For the first time since reaching their table, Tim turned his complete attention to Candy and Bill Walsh. "You mean to say," he asked, "you don't know?"

"Why, whatever do you mean?" Candy asked. "Of course we don't know. We have no idea at all."

"That's right," Walsh barked. "That monkey business back on the trail is over and done with now. Hell, Candy and me, we believe in letting bygones be bygones." He reached over and took Candy's hand. "Ain't that right, honey?"

She smiled sweetly at Bill, then turned her wide, innocent eyes on Winslow. "Bill and I are getting married tomorrow, right here in Seattle," she said. "There's a real nice Judge Maynard who's going to perform the ceremony."

Watching Bill Walsh closely, Winslow saw the man wince and wondered for a moment if the fellow hadn't lost a bet or something to make him take on for life such a treacherous tart. Suddenly Tim grabbed Winslow's arm and with a quick nod of his head, indicated the door. Winslow turned.

Standing in the doorway was Deacon Smathers.

"Now, you let me handle this," Walsh said as the deacon started for their table. "It won't take me long to tell that Bible thumper what's what."

But Winslow didn't think it was going to be so easy for Bill to handle Smathers—not with that look of pure hatred blazing in the deacon's eyes.

With barely a nod at Winslow, Smathers pulled up in front of the table, his eyes fixed on Candy.

Candy couldn't prevent herself from taking just one more potshot at the man. "Hello, Paul!" she sang. "Fancy meeting you in a place like this."

Smathers smiled—a hideous smile—and reached under his frock coat and pulled out the same revolver he had used to kill Thomas Grant. As he aimed the weapon at Candy, Winslow lifted the edge of the table and heaved it at Candy and Bill Walsh, knocking them both to the floor. As they hit, the deacon began firing, the detonations filling the saloon with thunder.

Tim threw himself at Smathers, but the man ducked aside, took another shot at the two on the floor, then turned and bolted from the room. Someone tried to stop him from leaving, but the deacon flung a wild shot at him and disappeared through the batwings. The shocked silence broke as the saloon patrons stampeded to the door. Before Winslow or Tim could push their way through the crush, however, there was a fusillade of shots outside.

Elbowing his way through the crowd on the sidewalk, Winslow saw the deacon. He was in the middle of Skid Road, lying face down in the mud with two loggers standing over him. One of them had a smoking Colt in his hand. The other was holding his arm as blood streamed through his fingers.

This second fellow looked up as Winslow and Tim ran over to Smathers. "That feller was loco!" he cried. "He just started shootin' at me!"

"You hurt bad?" Tim asked.

"Naw, just a flesh wound. But I'm not so sure about that feller. Sam caught him in the gut."

Winslow knelt in the mud beside Smathers and gently turned him over. Out of a face black with mud, the deacon's wide, unblinking eyes stared up at him. It was the first time Winslow had seen Smathers without his glasses on.

Without thinking, Winslow plucked the glasses out of the mud. The wire frame was twisted out of shape. He stood up and tossed the glasses away. Deacon Smathers wouldn't be needing them anymore.

* * *

A cadaverous individual dressed in black, with a white shirt and black string tie, hurried over, doffed his black bowler, and introduced himself as Asa Donner, the local mortician.

"Is this poor unfortunate your friend?" the undertaker asked Winslow.

"You might say that."

The man clasped his hands in relief. "May I suggest that you allow me to . . . attend to the sad details."

"Yes," Winslow said, turning on his heels. "Do it."

As Winslow and Tim approached the saloon, the crowd parted and Winslow saw a badly shaken Candy and Bill Walsh standing in the doorway. There wasn't a scratch on either of them, though Candy's hair was a bit mussed.

"You saved our lives!" Bill cried excitedly. "You pushed us out of the line of fire! That madman might have killed us!"

"Do me a favor—both of you," Winslow ordered.

"Of course. Of course," Bill agreed. "Anything you say, Winslow."

"Don't get married here in Seattle. Get married in Olympia."

"Olympia?"

"You heard me. And I want you to leave now."

"Now?"

"Yes. Now!"

Walsh looked a bit more closely at Winslow's cold eyes and swallowed. He nodded hastily. "Sure, Winslow. We don't like this place anyway. We'll leave right away. Tonight."

Tim Curry watched the two hurry off, then turned to Winslow.

"That undertaker probably wants a bundle to bury the preacher. How much do you have?"

"Not much," Winslow admitted. "But I know someone who can afford it. All during that trip from Baker, the preacher did what he could to make Kate feel uncomfortable—but that won't cut any ice with Kate. She'll do what she can to help us give him a decent sendoff." Scott looked sharply at Tim, then added, "Want to come along? That is, if you don't mind seeing Terry Lambert again."

"Why do you think I volunteered to come after Smathers?" Tim grinned as he followed Winslow down the street.

Now, as Tim hurried to keep up with Winslow's long strides, he came to a sudden decision that maybe wasn't all that sudden. He knew he should have spoken his feeling to Terry back in Oregon when he had the chance. Well, this time he wasn't going to hold back. He no longer was ashamed or afraid of what he felt for the young woman. And he didn't care what Terry said or how she protested—or what she had done in the past to survive. He was going to marry her and take her back to that rich Oregon valley with him.

Abruptly, he smiled. He had a pretty good idea that Terry wouldn't protest all that much.

For his part, Winslow had already decided to cash in his ticket to San Francisco. Seattle was raw, but it had a future. He could feel it in the air of the place. And he had an even more important reason for staying in Seattle: Kate Harrow. He had realized it the moment Candy had spoken ill of Kate. Her words had made him furious—with Candy and with himself. For if Candy was a hypocrite, what did that make him? He should have had the courage long before to admit that he loved and respected Kate Harrow.

Yes, he knew that he loved her, and somehow he was going to prove it to her. And then, if Kate would have him, Scott would help her turn that house on a hill into a home.

★ WAGONS WEST ★

A series of unforgettable books that trace the lives of a dauntless band of pioneering men, women, and children as they brave the hazards of an untamed land in their trek across America. This legendary caravan of people forge a new link in the wilderness. They are Americans from the North and the South, alongside immigrants, Blacks, and Indians, who wage fierce daily battles for survival on this uncompromising journey—each to their private destinies as they fulfill their greatest dreams.

☐	22808	**INDEPENDENCE!**	$3.50
☐	22784	**NEBRASKA!**	$3.50
☐	23177	**WYOMING!**	$3.50
☐	22568	**OREGON!**	$3.50
☐	23168	**TEXAS!**	$3.50
☐	23381	**CALIFORNIA!**	$3.50
☐	23405	**COLORADO!**	$3.50
☐	20174	**NEVADA!**	$3.50
☐	20919	**WASHINGTON!**	$3.50
☐	22952	**MONTANA!**	$3.95
☐	23572	**DAKOTA!**	$3.95